SAGA
of
GENERATIONS

SAGA
of
GENERATIONS

ADELE SINOWAY-BARNETT

Copyright © 2022 by Adele Sinoway-Barnett.

Library of Congress Control Number: 2022917335
ISBN: Hardcover 978-1-6698-4790-8
Softcover 978-1-6698-4789-2
eBook 978-1-6698-4788-5

All rights reserved. No part of this book may be reproduced or transmitted in any form or by any means, electronic or mechanical, including photocopying, recording, or by any information storage and retrieval system, without permission in writing from the copyright owner.

This is a work of fiction. Names, characters, places and incidents either are the product of the author's imagination or are used fictitiously, and any resemblance to any actual persons, living or dead, events, or locales is entirely coincidental.

Any people depicted in stock imagery provided by Getty Images are models, and such images are being used for illustrative purposes only.
Certain stock imagery © Getty Images.

Print information available on the last page.

Rev. date: 09/20/2022

To order additional copies of this book, contact:
Xlibris
844-714-8691
www.Xlibris.com
Orders@Xlibris.com
843439

CONTENTS

Russia 1

    1819 3
    1820 5
    1839 14
    1842 19
    1844 23

David's Rehabilitation 158

Hymie 164

Influenza Outbreak 169

Going Home 178

About The Author 189

About The Book 191

For my Family

RUSSIA

"Dirty Jew." As Zelda lay there huddled on the floor after being beaten so badly that her face felt like a pulp, he then raped her. She remained perfectly still, afraid to move. He then kicked her in the stomach. With a laugh, the man jumped on this horse and rode away to find his next victim. This was the second attack in one week. The year was 1818, and as Zelda lay crying and bleeding, she tried to stand, her knees buckling beneath her. She edged her way back to the village, seeing in front of her such devastation.

Small groups were beginning to form to discuss the day's horror, for to be found in larger numbers than three to four, one could expect to be flogged to death. Houses were burning, people were running to and fro, others were just standing, looking stunned, counting their blessings that their immediate family was all right. This time there had only been two deaths. Poor Mordecai, the village tailor, when he had tried to protect his wife, had been thrown aside and had knocked his head on the stone fireplace then beaten to death whilst his wife was about to be raped by five burly youths.

As each passed the bottle of vodka to the next, they smacked their lips in anticipation of the next prize of the beautiful Sarah, who but six months previously had married Mordecai. Now she found herself stretched out on the bed, with her arms and legs tied. Having been forced to watch the death of her husband, she saw the first youth approaching her unbuckling his belt and letting his gutkas (trousers) fall to the floor. Crying hysterically, she felt the searing pain shooting through her as he pushed into her. Another youth started fondling and kissing her breast. An unintelligible whisper of a voice was trying to emerge, pleading with them to leave her, until her mind and body could not accept what was happening anymore, and she thankfully slipped into unconscious oblivion. After each of the youths had their enjoyment and had no further use for her, they left her with a special present they said she would always remember them by: they cut off her right breast.

This was how the village elders had found her, as they made their tour from house to house checking on what damage had been done. They placed her on a makeshift stretcher, and she was taken to the barn that they had turned into an emergency hospital, but she was never to recover again. Her mutilated and bleeding body lay limp on the stretcher, and they had nothing that could help her.

Hearing the news as she arrived, Zelda hurried as best she could to the barn, only to confirm that this had actually happened to her best friend. Screaming, "Oh God, don't let it be true," she collapsed on the floor. Her rape today had brought on the first pains of labor as her firstborn child was due any time.

1819

Quiet and calm had spread over the village after the last pogrom. They were just fifteen miles north of Kiev. Things now were more on an even keel. Atrocities were being reported daily farther south, but one had to thank God and live from day to day. Some of the younger people had spoken of escape from this life, and some had even attempted to make the long and treacherous journey to the strange lands beyond.

Each village had its trade, and unless one managed to obtain a special travel pass, it was very dangerous to try to travel from one place to another.

Women were busy preparing for the festive holiday of Rosh Hashana when they saw from afar a rider drawing a cart behind him, Straining their eyes, they saw a gigantic vat, and as they recognized who it was, word went quickly around. Zelda rushed out with their now one-year-old infant son. Feeling herself sway and feeling faint with excitement, she fell into his wonderful strong arms.

Myer had managed to obtain a special travel pass so that he could travel to the Balkans, just before little Dov was born and therefore had never seen the child. The air filled with such excitement. As her stomach was churning into knots, she was filled with tremendous sadness that her friends Sarah and Mordecai would never share the happiness she felt. She pined so much for Sarah as she did not have any family in this village, as theirs, like most of the others, was an arranged marriage.

The long-awaited time until she was in Myer's arms again was like an eternity. First, he had to go through the expected ritual of greeting the elders and to tell them of his travels, how he had indeed acquired the enormous vat that was going to bring riches to both his family and to the village. He had paid out all the money the elders had collectively given him to two brothers he had met in Germany. They assured him that they could make him the best-quality vat, which would stand up to years and years of glue making in large quantities so the whole village would be involved.

Zelda in the meantime rushed to her neighbor. "Please, Mrs. Marks, could you look after Dov for a while? I must go to the mikvah. Myer is home." Without looking back, Zelda rushed off for the cleansing sacred waters of the baths. Late into the night and lying in the security of his safe strong arms, crying, she told him of the terrible experience she had before little Dov was born.

"Thank God, my little angel, you are here to tell of this and that he was born unharmed. If I could get my hands on that bastard, I would kill him. My anger for what they did to you is insurmountable."

1820

Winter had come and gone, and as evidenced everywhere, spring was here at last. Zelda, heavy with child, went to collect little Dov from Mrs. Zimmerman, who was in charge of the babies and toddlers of the village. Kissing him fondly and looking at a picture he had drawn, she just loved the way he chattered and tried to tell her all he had done during the course of one day, in five minutes!

"Now tell me, Dov, what would you like Momma to make you for dinner? I have lovely chicken soup and chicken." She knew this was his favorite.

"Yes, please, Momma." As he ran down the path to their home, he felt released from the fat Mrs. Zimmerman's strict ruling as when in her care, no one dared be rude and at all times treated her with the utmost respect. And young as he was, he had learned very quickly that all hell broke loose and you could be made to spend most of the day facing the corner.

"I know how much you do not like going to the nursery, my precious darling, but I have to try to help your papa. I have to work collecting wood and stack the cart." She knew this was impossible for him to understand as he was still far too young. Her work was hard; she helped Myer to load, and once that was done, she would sit on top to keep the logs balanced so they did not come off.

It was backbreaking for Myer too. His horse was becoming old as it pulled the cart. "My darling Zelda, I see how it is increasingly harder for you to do this type of work," he had told her. "And you are soon with child. Tomorrow I want you to rest."

"Myer, you just don't understand how we are facing such hard times, for as hard as we work, they want more and more taxes from us. Only last week, they made an example of Mr. Aronowitz, who raises chickens, and because he did not produce as many eggs as was expected of him, they schlepped [dragged] him off and beat him." Her baby inside her was kicking viciously as if in protest, so she told Myer she would see him at home later.

As she was reminiscing about today's happenings, she again called on Mrs. Marks to watch over little Dov whilst she went to the mikvah, and on her return, she bathed him and saw he was watching her setting the candles in their holders, for tonight was the Sabbath. Everything was in readiness for Myer's return from work as when the sun began to set, the Shabbas began. For the following day, as her mother before her had done, Zelda had fried fish so she would not have to cook, and sometimes especially if the family was going to join them, she made a cholent, but this she liked especially in the winter: meat, potatoes, and barley simmering in the oven all night and during the morning of the following day. But she had to have the cholent cooked in the community bakery along with the other villagers that chose to make this dish. Their cooking means were extremely primitive. All Zelda had was a range, which was to be envied by some, but to get heat out of it, one had to feed it continuously with little sticks of wood; therefore, it was impossible to cook anything like a cholent in one's own home,

Myer's form cut out the light in the doorway, as he stood for a moment with pride, watching his wife and child. As Dov saw him, he screamed with excitement. Myer drew him up in his arms and swung him around, after which his arm went around Zelda. He gave her a kiss and an extra pat on her tummy. "Just so he knows his papa is home—why should he be left out of it?" he joked laughingly.

After bathing, Myer, now refreshed from his hard day's work, watched Zelda put her scarf on and cover her eyes, praying as she lit the candles. Her hands encircling the flames held such a fascination for Dov that when she finished, he asked, "Why do you do that, Momma?"

Zelda replied in a very soft voice. "It is to pray to God to keep us all well within this home." And so their Shabbas dinner began.

Zelda felt her time was drawing near. It was an effort to turn over in bed, and as Myer lay snoring, she decided to get up early. She was already getting niggling pains low down for the past few days, her back was aching, and all she could think of was how Myer was going to manage without her help. Waking Dov, she gave him his morning milk and bread, by which time Myer was up and having his wash. There was no running water in the shtetl (home); this was brought in by Myer the night before.

"Hello, my darling," Zelda said as she held her back. Myer gave his usual grunt, impossible to speak to him in the mornings, but remembering the conversation she had with her friend Hannah only last week when she cried to her that her husband without any thought for her mauled at her body like an animal waking her out of a deep sleep just to relieve himself, never a sign of affection or feeling for her, and when she thought she would say no, he started hitting her, which seemed to get him even more excited, so now she suffered in silence. Zelda, bearing this in mind, thought how lucky she had been in her marriage to Myer. He was such a gutte neshuma (good person).

Daydreaming as she walked along, Zelda deposited Dov with Mrs. Zimmerman and, promptly at 7:00 a.m., entered the yard with the hustle and bustle of the other workers going about their various duties, when she saw Myer excitedly speaking to his sister's husband Shmuel (Samuel), who had brought a message from Myer's mother that she could not help them today as she had a bad back. Zelda groaned and moaned to herself as the cart pulled out of the yard, more work for her to do as her mother-in-law had eased things a little for her these past few weeks.

"My precious one, look at you. Here, have some water." Myer put his arm around her, showing his concern. Looking into her eyes, he promised that things would soon be easier for her. "I have told my oldest nephew that now that he has had his bar mitzvah, he can come to work for me as an apprentice."

Finally, they had piled the logs as high as they dared, Myer helped Zelda up until she was on top of them and then he proceeded to urge the old horse to move forward. Their long journey seemed like a never-ending nightmare, feeling every curve and bump in the road. Sweat started streaming down her face. Taking her hands off the logs, she wiped herself. The cart jolted, and Zelda, losing her balance, began to fall.

Hearing her scream, Myer was as if paralyzed but forced himself over to her.

"Our baby, Myer, please save the baby." He fell to his knees. With her head cradled in his arms, he did not know what to do, for to leave her now and get help would take at least two hours. His only hope was that someone would happen along the path.

"Hold on, my darling. Everything will be all right. I will not leave you. Someone will come along. I love you. I have never told you, but you have become more to me than life itself. I need you, Dov needs you. Hold my hand. I am here for you."

In the meantime, Zelda's face was twisting in agony, her hand grasping his every time the pain overwhelmed her. Then from a distance, Myer could see another cart coming their way.

"Someone is coming, my love, someone is coming. We will soon get you home, and you will be all right." Myer laid her head on his jacket and started running toward the other traveler. When he had explained what happened, they suggested that as their cart was practically empty, they lay Zelda down in it and they would take them back to their village so they could at least get help.

They carried Zelda very carefully into Myer's shtetl, which he with the help of his family had built just before his marriage and consisted of two rooms. Mrs. Zuckerman had been a midwife for more years than she cared to remember, and she immediately came running over. "Oy vey [oh my goodness], my poor child, you try to rest. I'll be back soon. I'm going to send my son to bring the doctor."

Myer remained by Zelda's side throughout the journey and stayed mopping her brow and listening to her fevered hallucinations for two days and two nights until finally the only doctor from five villages away was able to come to see her. He told Myer, "Unless I perform an incision, I cannot save the baby. But because of a breech position, you may lose both, as the mother's fall brought on the labor and this is now weakening her heart." The doctor was quite definite about this. Shocked, Myer nodded his consent. The doctor went back into the bedroom. "Mrs. Zuckerman, scrub the table and boil water." Turning to Zelda, he said, "You will soon be sitting up, holding your infant."

Mrs. Zuckerman went over to Zelda, smiling and patting her hand as Zelda, with tears streaming down her face, looked up at her with frightened eyes. "Do not worry. I am here and I will be with you all the time."

To Zelda, the doctor said, "You've had a complete shock to your system, child, but we'll soon put you right," and then he left the room.

Pacing up and down, tears streaming down his face, Myer realized that he could forever lose his sweet Zelda, blurred from his tears he stumbled, found himself a chair, and buried his head between his knees. "Please let this be a dream, I am surely going to wake up and it's not going to be true" and so he sat for what seemed an eternity until he felt the presence of someone else in the room.

Coming toward him was the doctor, his face very solemn. The doctor shook his head and said, "I'm so sorry, Myer. I did my best for your wife, but her heart was not strong enough after all she'd been through. We managed to save the child, a girl, may her dear mother rest in peace. I will get the rabbi for you. Rest now. I'm so sorry."

The rabbi called on them. He spoke highly of Zelda, saying she was a gutte neshuma (meaning she was a good person). "She always attended our services, even in these difficult times. She was an excellent example for the younger members of the community to follow." He arranged with Myer for the funeral to be set for the following day at 2:00 p.m., in order for Zelda's family to have enough time to arrive.

Preparation had to be made for little Dov. Myer's sister Rebecca (Becky, as she was called as a child) and her husband Samuel did not have any children. They were only too pleased to care for Dov, whom they loved, and the child was used to them. They volunteered to look after the new baby too. Myer sat there like a statue, staring into space. "Thank you, thank you, I have no words to say. My life is empty, and my beautiful Zelda would be thanking you too if she could. One thing I insist on, the baby must according to tradition carry Zelda's name, but as this will be a constant reminder to me, I will only give the child her initial, so her name will be Zena."

Word had been sent by a messenger, and the morning brought new sorrow for Myer. Along the dusty dirt road to the village trailed Zelda's mother, four sisters, three brothers, two uncles, and three aunts, some cousins, and three of her six nephews, as those that had not been bar mitzvahed could not attend the funeral. Myer embraced them, and so the two families came together under such tragic circumstances. Zelda's mother shouted hysterically, "Where is she? I want to be with her." Sobbing, they were led into what had been Zelda's home, and there right in front of them lay the coffin draped with a black cloth facing the door. On the side were two candles and a Yahrzeit (memorial) light, which was to be lit after the funeral.

The room had been sparsely furnished, but now lining the walls were nine shiva chairs, which according to tradition were low seats the family were to sit on during the mourning period. They crowded around the coffin. Myer went over to his mother-in-law and put his arm around her. Sobbing, she looked up at him and then touched the coffin, rested her head on the box, clutching each side. "If there is a God in heaven, I'm asking you why didn't he take me?" she moaned. "Why did I have to live to see my own daughter dead?" She was getting hysterical, which was making it harder for everyone else to bear.

Outside, all the men from the village were standing around in little groups when the signal went around it was time. The cart had been drawn up outside. Myer took his place next to the coffin, alongside Zelda's three brothers and three nephews. The women had been urged to move to the side of the room. Sympathetically, they clutched at one another, not daring to look as Zelda's body was taken out of her home for the very last time.

Slowly, the funeral procession reached the burial grounds, which was but a short distance away, and as the rabbi prayed and asked for Kaddish to be said (a special prayer for the dead), tears welled up uncontrollably in Myer. "My love, I will never forget you." And with that, he threw himself on the ground and sobbed until his brother-in-law Samuel eased him up and put his arms around him, then each person put a shovel full of earth onto the grave.

1839

Dov, now a handsome young man, had thankfully escaped each marriage match arranged for him. Every time his father suggested someone, he said he was seriously thinking of moving on and didn't want to be encumbered with a wife.

After his mother had died, his Aunt Becky and Uncle Samuel had practically brought up both his sister Zena and him. His father had waited out the traditional year of mourning and then as was the custom had married his mother's younger sister Ruth, who from the beginning showed that this was not her idea of marriage. Contempt of Myer was so strong that the only way she could let her temper out was with the children, so Dov soon learned to keep well away from her. Every opportunity both children had, they could be found around the lovable Aunt Becky, who taught them all she knew, and what she didn't know she found out for them.

Ruth did bear Myer four sons, and although Myer loved all his children, his little Zena was the apple of his eye. Looking back on the fact that he now had four half brothers, it made Dov wonder how this ever came about. They were certainly not born of love but only when her protests were no longer excusable. Myer accepted his life for what it was; he had always found a willing partner in Zelda, but now he had been rejected so often by Ruth that the urge to make love had subsided to a now very occasional thing.

They came together to bed with never a thought of making love but only to sleep. Ruth always had a headache, a stomachache, or a backache. If Myer was a gambling man, he would have bet on which one it was going to be that night. His thoughts often turned to his life as it had been. Although he always tried to look ahead, it was with a feeling of sadness and joy that he saw Zena grow into a beautiful young woman, very similar in looks to how Zelda had been. However, it was now drawing near to the time that he had agreed to her marriage to a young man from the nearby village of Polotsk.

"Time waits for no one, Zena, my love. I want you to get together with Becky, get some of the other women to help you. I want my daughter to go out of here and into her new life having a wonderful day for us all to remember." Zena was looking at her father in awe. There was no questioning him on his decision for her. She had only seen a glimpse of her husband. He looked handsome, and she was flattered that she was to be his wife.

"Ruth, I think Saul Rifkoff after all will make her a good husband. I saw his father yesterday, and he told me he has now finished his apprenticeship as a builder and he has already got a little home together for them to start off their lives. I told him I would speak to the rabbi and arrange all the festivities."

Excitement stirred in the village of Dvinsk. Saul was a prize catch, handsome and strong. Becky was so excited she took Zena to the mikvah, which had sacred waters that had been blessed, so she might cleanse her body thoroughly before entering under the chuppah. This was a canopy that had been erected in a field nearby and under which the couple would have their ceremony.

All the tables were set with food, and as the congregation gathered around, Zena on the arm of her father felt herself trembling. Myer's hand went to hers, patted it, and with tears in his eyes, he said, "This is the proudest day of my life. God bless you both," as he gently led her toward her waiting groom.

As she stood under the chuppah, her veil covering her face, Zena, who had briefly met Saul once, saw now just the side of the face of the man the rabbi was joining her to. Saul took her hand and placed the ring on it. Her veil was lifted, and he gave her a light kiss on the lips. It was all as if it were happening to someone else, like a dream, and as the service was coming to an end, Saul stepped on the glass and everyone around them shouted, "Mazel tov!"

Zena's eyes looked around for her father. "Poppa," Zena said in a choked voice as he put his arms around her and hugged her. Ruth was next in line, and as she bent and gave her a light kiss on the cheek, all the bitterness she had felt for her stepmother in the past welled up in her and for the first time she felt a closeness as she realized that she didn't have any choice in her marriage the same as she. Come what may though, it was up to the individual to accept one's fate.

"I'm sorry, Ruth, that we didn't get on too well. Maybe we could have gotten on better if I had tried to understand. All I can tell you is I'm so frightened."

Ruth put her arm around her and said, "He's handsome, young, and strong. Look how he's looking at you. I should be the one to apologize to you. My poor sister, may she lie in peace, would be so happy today if she could see you. She was very much in love with your father. Forced as I was to marry him, I have had to live in her shadow, with comparisons thrown in my face all through my marriage. Dear Zena, for you, things will be different. Don't be frightened but give yourself to him as though you are one, and I truly wish you every happiness."

Throughout the eating and drinking, Myer had hired three musicians to serenade them. As they came among the guests, playing their violins, the festive atmosphere started to erupt. Holding their handkerchiefs between them, the men started dancing around one table. Saul was held high on a chair held by a few strong guests. Dancing, the women, also with handkerchiefs between them, took hold of Zena on her chair, forming a circle until the two chairs were close enough for them to hold their handkerchiefs between them.

When they were finally on their own, their journey back to Saul's village was very tiring after such an exciting day they had left all the festivities still in progress among a lot of backslapping and laughter among the men. Among the women, Aunt Becky was crying like she was a lamb going to slaughter, and as she held her, Zena wanted to cry out, as every instinct was to hold on to her like she did when she was a child for her to save her when there was anything going on she did not like.

Now, everyone a distant vision, she still turned round to give them the last wave, when Saul looked at her and said, "You are very beautiful. I hope we'll be happy together. It was a wonderful wedding. Now today, tomorrow, and the days after, we are one, you and I, Zena."

Finally arriving in their new shtetl, he took her in his arms for the very first time, kissing her face and neck. He cupped her face in his hands and kissed her on her eyes and nose. "Don't be frightened of me, Zena. I will not hurt you. We are both young and inexperienced, so we will learn together and we have all our lives to do so."

For the first time that day, Zena felt more relaxed. He was very sweet and certainly very handsome, this new husband of hers, and hard to explain the most tingling sensations running through her as he kissed her, but most of all, when he had told her not to be frightened of him, it made her realize that he must be just as nervous as she.

"I will give you privacy, Zena. You go in and prepare for bed." After washing, putting on her nightdress, and brushing her hair, she knocked on the door. When there was no answer, she peeped round the door. There in bed was Saul, his arms resting behind his head. Pulling the cover down on Zena's side, he said, "Come, my love, join me."

1842

Night had drawn on. Most had already retired to bed when doors were flung open and the inhabitants were dragged out, some screaming, most resisting, but those that did were instantly clubbed to death.

Orders were to punish the Jewish population in the area for not meeting their taxes, although they had been set extraordinarily high. There was no hope of meeting them. An example had to be made so they would work harder in the future.

Mrs. Zimmerman, now getting on in years, heard the commotion and came running out in the square, hitting whoever came into her path with a candlestick until someone grabbed hold of her and tied her to a cart. As they pulled it along, they whipped her. Each time she stumbled, she felt the whiplash against her back until they could do with her as they would, she felt no more as she had a massive heart attack.

Myer and his family were sleeping at that time, as were most when the pogrom started, and as they were being dragged from their beds, they kicked and swore, trying desperately to get free. Ruth they tied to her bed and laughingly set fire to it as she screamed to her death.

Myer and his four younger sons were clubbed unconscious and dragged to the village square, where their clothing was torn off them. "Cut those Jews up," the Cossack shouted, and so where their penises and testicles had been was nothing more than a bloody mess, and those that showed any sign of life had a sword thrust into them.

At that time, Dov was visiting his sister Zena, who had just given birth to her second daughter when word came through of all the terrible things that had happened. The very few survivors had been very descriptive, and word had soon been sent to the surrounding areas.

Dov waited for Saul to return from work as he and Zena had been in such a state of shock she was shaking from head to toe, with tears running down her face, that he said, "Saul, we must not sit back and let this happen to us. I would have been killed along with my family. Now I only have you, Zena, and the kleiner [children] to worry about. We must all pack up as little as possible and get out of here. It is time to go." Saul had been talking to Zena about this throughout their marriage, but now he saw and felt the determination on his beloved's face.

"Saul, I must protect my children. I want to go."

They managed to get travel passes, their belongings piled as high as they dared they had secured a donkey and a cart, and although it was raining and they were miserable, their emotions ran high. Dov did not go back to Dvinsk, and they set out on their journey from Polotsk, Zena was singing softly to the baby whom she had named after her mother Zelda. Her daughter Hannah was leaning against her, fast asleep. "Saul, I thank God that we are away from this place. I cannot believe that my whole family has been wiped out in such a horrible, vicious way." Her voice broke into faint sobs.

Saul put his arm around her. "Soon, soon, my love, we will be able to start a new life, a new home, and everything we need." So their journey began and was long and tedious.

It rained as, wearily, they traveled on. Hungry and wet right through, they approached a farm. They stopped the cart at the boundary, and politely, Dov and Saul knocked on the farmer's door, asking permission to stay overnight in his barn, showing him their travel passes.

He waved them on. "Make sure you are gone by first light. I don't want the reputation that I keep Jews here."

Thankfully, they managed to snatch a few hours' sleep. The meager food they had brought with them was now running out, but along the way, they managed to dig up some potatoes, and if nothing else, it sustained the hunger pangs. Nights drifted into days. Baby Zelda cried and cried, and as Zena felt the baby's keppalah (head), it felt hot with fever. "Saul, we must stop for a while. I have to have a chance to tend to the children. We are all exhausted, and the baby is not doing well. My milk must have dried up. I don't think she's getting anything." Hannah, a little toddler herself, was fast asleep, nestled up against her mother.

Spotting a farm in the distance, they stopped to ask if the farmer needed any help, and as he did, they were thankful to say they would stop for a week. Dov and Saul, both strapping young men, set to work fixing fences and plowing the fields. One week turned into one month. Both the children had developed chickenpox; as one finished, the other started. Each day the farmer was so good to them, giving them fruit, vegetables, and a few live chickens, which they killed as and when they needed. Zena did wonders with the food and each day strolled down to the stream and caught some fish, which she smoked and stored, plus whatever chickens they did not eat were fed and kept in anticipation for their expected journey, for to take them alive would be far healthier, and with luck, they would have the eggs, which would be good for the children.

They worked hard, and so far so good. The farmer and his wife were sorry to see them go but, on their departure, came out to wave them off. "You are both good men, and we have become fond of your lovely family." His wife came forward and put her arms around Zena's shoulders. Then to their surprise, the couple's young son came from behind the barn with a cow. "For the children, God be with you."

1844

After crossing over the border of Russia, they were on the outskirts of Bialystok, Poland. First thing was to find a synagogue and ask the rabbi for help, which they did, and he invited them to stay over until they could find work, which they were very grateful for, and Zena was pregnant with her third baby, so the rest for her was very important right now.

One of the merchants gave Dov a job working in his store. Saul found a job in carpentry, which he knew only too well. Time went on and their stay turned into two years, and Dov found himself more and more in love with his employer's daughter Anna, the most beautiful girl he had ever seen. Approaching her father, Dov told him how much he loved his daughter. "I love her, sir. I know I am nine years her senior, but I will try to give her everything humanly possible and I beg you, sir, for your daughter's hand in marriage."

Her father screamed at him, "Are you crazy? A *nothing* asks for my daughter to marry him. You could never provide for her what she deserves. All you can think of is this thing throbbing in your pants. You are not thinking of the welfare of my daughter. No, never, never!"

Devastated, Dov went back to his sister Zena and brother-in-law and told them the outcome of the conversation. "She is the only woman for me. I will ask Anna to run away with me as quickly as possible before her father sends her off to her aunt in a different town as he has threatened."

Waiting for Anna as she came out of her father's shop, he told her of her father's decision "Please, Anna, come away with me. I love you to madness. We'll go to Paris, and no one will ever keep us apart."

Looking into his eyes, she said, "I love you, Dov, and I will go to the end of the world with you." So it was decided that she would slip out of her home that evening and Dov would be waiting for her and they would go as quickly as possible.

Rushing back to Zena and Saul, he told them of this news. He promised that as soon as he would get to Paris, he would get a place for them to come too. In between, they promised to try to learn the French language. They now had their three beautiful children Hannah, Zelda, and Leon, and hoped for no more; they felt their little family was complete.

Stealthily in the night, they took their departure, fearing the girl's father might hear them. Dov, then thirty-one, promised, "My darling Anna, as soon as we are able to, we will find a rabbi and get married, because my love flows for you like a fountain. I can never remember when I have felt so happy in my whole life."

Although it was their intention to wait until the rabbi married them, they lay in each other's arms that night with nature all around them. Dov whispered in Anna's ears, "Please, Anna, we are to be married anyway. I can hardly contain myself. I love you so much I can't wait. I need you now, not in six weeks or six months, but now."

The curve of her body nestled closer to him as in an invitation, and as his lips found hers, his tongue entered her mouth. And as her tongue came out to meet his, the emotional sensation came rising within him. Anna was clinging to him as he parted her legs. "Relax, my love." Slowly he eased himself into her as she stifled a scream into his shoulder. "Relax, relax, it is all right, darling. It will be all right now. I love you so much," he told her as he quickly reached an orgasm. "Next time it will be better, you'll see, and it will not hurt. It is only because it is the first time for you."

Anna lay crying softly. "I'll be all right soon. It is just the reaction of everything. I only wish that things were different with my parents and we could have been married first."

"We are now married in the eyes of God. Just think of that, my love, and you had better get used to me, for I will love you to death."

So their togetherness began, not like most couples in their matrimonial beds, but in a field under the stars.

Once they had finally reached Paris, Dov found a rabbi to marry them. Anna had given birth to their son Yossel in very primitive conditions whilst they were still traveling. It was so hard for them as they had no money and were scrimping all the way, Dov finding a day's work here and there to buy food for the following day and, if they were lucky, being allowed to stay in the barn of a friendly farmer, but being in love and only having each other to care about until Yossel came along. Dov, now looking back, thought of them as exciting days.

Sending word to both their families that they had arrived in Paris and had been married by a rabbi, but then to Anna's dismay, there was never a word from her parents. It was as if she did not exist. One day, her younger brother decided to make a break from his overbearing father and look up his beloved sister. Judah came and stayed for a while until he found employment and finally married. The newly married couple moved to a farm just on the outskirts of Paris, and although he worked hard, he always tried every few weeks to come and visit, bringing with him a sack of potatoes, which was gratefully accepted.

Dov, it seemed, was continually looking for employment, so when he entered the door, he burst in with pride. "At last I have found something I will be good at." He had applied for a job in a glue factory and he had told them of the training he had with his father, and this had put him in good stead. "I have the job."

With so many mouths to feed, it seemed like Anna was forever pregnant, but the feel of her body next to him at night awakened his desires and they enjoyed a good sex life together. Anna understood this man of hers needed a lot of love and affection, but she too craved his touch, with exciting vibrations coming into her being together with longings to be enveloped in his arms and feel him harden and enter her.

Happiness seemed complete. His precious Anna was in the background cutting up long strips of lokshen (vermicelli, pasta) and hanging it to dry when Dov gathered his seven children around him and said, "Word has just come through from my sister Zena that at last, they are able to make the long journey here. Her daughters Zelda and Hannah are now married and are traveling with their husbands. Her son Leon passed away a year ago. Zelda has a son three months old and has named him Solomon, taking the initial of her father Saul, who died two years ago, God rest his dear soul."

Anna gathered round with her children to listen too, now expecting another child in just a few months. Dov continued, "It has been very rough for my family, and this is the only family I have so, kinder, when they do arrive, we must all try to make them feel at home. My poor sister Zena must have been heartbroken when her husband and then her son died." He looked at Anna. "I understand Saul had been ill for some time, and although she nursed him, there was nothing more she could do, and then on top of it to lose a child. Anna, I know how difficult it will be for us, but they will share our space until such time as they find their own."

"Dov, how can we put up so many people? We cannot move around as it is in three rooms." Anna was looking at him in amazement at what he was saying, and getting quite angry. She had never had any association with this Zena and here he was pushing his whole family on her in her condition with soon another mouth to feed. Well, that was Dov, and after all this time, she knew whatever he decided, that was how it must be.

Zena clutched the paper with the address, although she had memorized Rue de Ferdinand. "We are here. At last, we have arrived." She knocked on apartment door 56, and there in front of her was her beloved brother. She fell into his arms, with tears streaming down everyone's faces. He was overwhelmed to introduce the family to each other. The smell of the chicken soup cooking and the chicken in the oven made a wonderful feeling of welcome.

Anna stepped forward to give her sister-in-law a big hug and said, "Come, I will show you to your room. Take off your coats and the kleiner [children] can eat first." Yossel, Myer, Ada, Sarah, Bertha, Rifka, and Aaron all came forward to meet their aunt and cousins.

"Oh my, how wonderful, my tears are flowing with happiness," Zena said.

With the arrival of Zena and the family, life was very hectic in their three rooms. Dov allocated the largest to Zena, the two daughters, their husbands, and baby Solly, as they all began to call the new baby; however, no one seemed to mind all the upheaval. They were just pleased to have a roof over their heads.

"You can stay just as long as you want. When you find yourselves jobs, then look for somewhere to live, but in the meantime, you have a home," Dov told them, and Zena looked at her brother thankfully, with tears in her eyes.

Sanitary conditions were not the best. Washing seemed to be everywhere. With so many children around, it was inevitable. Each tried to bathe at least once a week. They had an enormous tin bath, which they had to fill with bowls of water. The tap was outside the building, and they had to carry the water up and then stoke the fire to boil it. Three children were bathed together. The same water with a top-up had to last for the rest of the children. Emptying the tub was another chore. The bath had to be tilted slowly into bowls and thrown down the sink, scrubbed out, and then the process started all over again.

Sectioning off a corner of the room with a curtain so they could bathe and have some privacy, they also had a bowl in there so each one could use it to have a stand-up wash each day. Toilet conditions were worse. The only toilet was shared with other apartments and was two flights down, so from necessity, the men used the toilet that was out in the street, and for the young children, they kept a pot handy.

Wearily climbing up the stairs one evening, Dov saw the children playing out on the landing near the doorway. He had a very hard day at work, but now that Zelda's husband Leon had found a job, things should be easier for them all. The children started chattering all at once as they saw him, so he held up his hand and said, "Such excitement, what is it, for goodness' sake?"

"We have a new baby brother, Poppa. He's just been born, and we are waiting to go in to see him."

Dov opened the door quietly, beaming proudly. The women that had been there with Anna all shouted, "Mazel tov," and there in front of him was his beautiful Anna holding their latest addition, who was airing his lungs and letting them all know he'd arrived in this big world. Approaching the bed, Dov put his arms around his wife, kissing her, stroking her face, and then his arms went out to his new infant son.

"He is beautiful like his mother, handsome like his father. With such a combination, how could anyone go wrong?" Dov jokingly told them all. "But, I do not know, Anna. I am already starting to run out of names. What shall we call this little fellow?"

"Let us call him Aaron. It is a good, solid name, Dov. Yes, Aaron Kohn sounds good." Looking lovingly down at the child as Dov placed him back in her arms, she nodded.

"You had an uncle by that name, Anna. Yes, well, this little one is now named after him. God rest his soul."

Gaining back her strength each day little by little, Anna began to make preparations for the baby's bris (circumcision), which was to be done traditionally on the eighth day after the baby had been born. Friends in the district had been invited, and Zena had helped in making the food so that they had a nice table laid by the time the mohel (not a doctor but a man specializing in circumcision) arrived, everyone else had gathered. The men gathered around the baby, and they placed a little wine over some cloth and let it drip into the baby's mouth. It was all over very quickly. "Mazel tov" was the general word between one another. The wine was passed around, and as they raised their glasses, Dov held up his hand, commanding attention.

"Not very often do I have the chance to make a speech, but today is a day when I feel I must. First, lehayim [to life]." And he took a sip of his wine. "I want to thank my friends and family, on behalf of my wife Anna, for being here today to celebrate this occasion. We have named our son Aaron, which means 'enlightener,' and who knows, maybe he will become a teacher." As everyone laughed, Dov raised his glass once again. "Lehayim."

Anna went over and gave Dov a kiss on the cheek. With a little tear in her eye, she said, "You know me, all sentimental."

Dov put his arm around Anna and said, "I have never been happier. My beautiful family and now my sister and her family are here. May we always have peace and good health."

Life was a hard struggle. If one was in Russia, Poland, and now France, it made no difference. You still had to work hard to put food on the table, but at least here there were no pogroms and one could bring their family up with peace of mind. Yes, there was still anti-Semitism and you heard "Jew" but nothing like they had experienced. Both Dov and Zena had lost their father Myer and his family in the most horrific way, so their memories of Russia were a nightmare and when they passed this knowledge down to their children, it was with such sadness, and yes, such happiness that they were all safe with them in Paris.

The year was 1862. Zena had joined her brother Dov and sister-in-law Anna in Paris, bringing with her two daughters Zelda, Leon, and baby Solomon (whom they all ended up calling first Solly and then Sol). Hannah and her husband Benjamin had nowhere to go other than to stay with Dov.

Leon was a very determined young man. He managed to get a job pushing out the traders' carts into the open street market and mainly those selling vegetables. When one of the other helpers did not turn up one morning, he said to the supervisor, "I have a brother-in-law that would be only too pleased with the work."

"Bring him then tomorrow at 5:00 a.m. sharp," the supervisor replied.

Going home full of excitement, Leon told Benjamin, "I got you a job working with me, and you must start tomorrow."

"I cannot say I am overjoyed doing that kind of work, Leon, but I realize we cannot live here forever, so I will take anything for now. Thank you for trying for me."

"Well, give it a chance. It is not too bad, and if you like it, the girls can then start to look around for somewhere for us to move into. We can all move together, but I will tell you one thing. I have just got to get Zelda and me into a bedroom of our own. You do not seem to be making out too bad because we can hear everything, but knowing we are all in the same room, especially our mother-in-law, I cannot even get an erection."

"Sex is not everything in a marriage," Benjamin said rather shyly.

"No, but it certainly helps, gunser knucker [big shot]. No time you have been married and so far you are getting a regular supply. Let us hear what you have got to say if and when you do not get it for a while. You will get like me a bear with a sore head." Leon, in a temper now, walked out to the street to cool down, mumbling to himself. It seemed this was all he was able to think of lately.

Shy and withdrawn, Benjamin was not at all like Leon but he loved Hannah and so he left his family in Russia. Things were really bad at that time. Jews were leaving their homes and abandoning all their possessions to just get away and to start a new life somewhere, anywhere—no one really cared; they just wanted a chance to live, but now of course, the everyday living was getting to him.

Yes, he made love to his beautiful wife, but as much as he tried to be quiet, how could one relax and enjoy the slightest movement? Even the bed creaked. He could not allow his seed to go into Hannah in case she moaned in ecstasy, and so to relieve himself, he ejaculated all over her stomach.

Both Benjamin and Leon worked hard. It was no easy task schlepping (pulling) those carts around, but finally to their joy, they arrived home to find their mother-in-law Zena busy with Solly and with a message: "The girls told me to tell you to meet them at Rue de Marseilles. I do not remember the number. I have it written down on the table over there . . . just under the ornament. Finding this apartment, they arranged to meet the owner back there so when you came home from work, you could both see it first and decide."

"What is there to decide, as long as we have got more room than we have here, all cramped into one room?" Leon anxiously said, looking from one to another. "Hurry up, Benjamin, let us go. We will not be long, Momma."

On the way to the apartment, Leon voiced his opinion about things once more.

"You know, I have been thinking, we are pushing those stinking carts around for the traders and earning next to nothing. Once we get ourselves out of that rat hole and feel we can breathe again, we should try to save for a bit of stock and try it on our own, rather than work for someone else and make them rich. Do not get me wrong. I am thankful for Uncle Dov and Aunt Anna to have had us and put up with a complete upheaval of their lives, but we have to stand on our own."

Benjamin, although a good worker, was a man of few words—a thinker, yes, but a speaker, no. He just nodded and smiled. Every day was a new thought for Leon, so Benjamin just learned to go along with all his ranting and raving and keep his mouth shut.

When they reached apartment #13, they found Hannah in tears because after searching all over Paris, this was the best they could come up with for the price they could afford. "Why are you crying?" Benjamin was immediately by her side, giving her a kiss on the cheek.

"Well, Momma's going to be so upset. She will think we do not want her, but look how small the rooms are." Hannah, very realistic and practical, knew that they must make the breakaway from her family. The only way to move was to share with Zelda and Leon. Financially, they could never do it on their own right now. "My poor Momma, after all she has been through, I cannot bear to think I'm leaving her."

Benjamin, now with his arms around her, patted her on her back. "Shh, darling, beautiful girl, she will not be far."

The apartment consisted of three small rooms, two of which could be used as bedrooms, the larger of course for Zelda as she had the baby Sol, so they definitely needed the extra space. The third room, if you could call it a room, consisted of a cupboard, a small table and chairs, a sink, and a range that had to be stoked up with wood or coal—this was a nice size and could actually hold four pots; however, there was hardly enough room to swing a cat around. They would have to eat in shifts.

"Let us take it. Otherwise, we will end up staying at Uncle Dov's forever, and you, my dear wife, will end up having to worry about me having a mistress somewhere! It is only a start, and yes, we can have Momma living with us later on." Leon could not contain his excitement.

They all agreed, paid the landlord his deposit, signed some papers he presented, and the apartment was then theirs. Leon, after the man had left, giving them their keys, swung Zelda into his arms and said, "At last, my little dove, you have escaped me long enough, caught in my trap, ho ho."

They all laughed and decided to head back to Uncle Dov's apartment. They needed to organize beds, which they hoped to do the following day, and then move in and get what they needed when they could. Really, they needed everything. Perhaps they could look in the meantime in some secondhand shops.

The following night, they were all in their separate rooms when Leon put his arms around Zelda, undoing her bra and immediately fondling and kissing her nipples. "I cannot tell you how I have waited for this evening, our own privacy."

As he continued to remove her clothing, she said, "Leon, be careful. The baby—"

"I will not hurt you or the baby. Just lie next to me, my love, and stroke me, hold me tight, and make me come. I need you so much, Zelda." As they lay there in each other's arms, Leon suddenly shook violently against her, but as he had not penetrated her, he saturated the sheets. Zelda immediately jumped up and put a towel underneath them, after which they both drifted off into a contented sleep.

They were able to accumulate some money, all living together. They shared whatever expense they had. Zena was still living with Dov, who was quite happy to have her as she got on so well with Anna and was a marvelous help with all the children.

Leon, bounding in from work one day, put his arms around Zelda's shoulders, looked her squarely in the face, and said, "Wish me mazel tov."

Looking at him in amazement, she replied, "So tell me what for, what is it, Leon? I never know with you what you are going to get up to next."

"Sit down, my sweet, take the weight off your feet. If you weren't so big, I'd take you to bed right now," he told her.

"A one-track mind you have, you want me to be like my Aunt Anna, always with a big belly, so nu?" (well) Impatiently, Zelda had an irritated tone in her voice.

"Benjamin and I have gone into business together. We have saved some money, not much, but a franc here and there, and we have bought ourselves a cart. Now we must work until we can save enough money to put some stock on it. We knew Mr. Gould wanted to retire, so we told him when he was ready, we would buy it off him. I tell you, Zelda, with Hannah only just falling pregnant, I was beginning to think that he did not know how to put it in right! Now they think it is twins, we decided we had better do something fast. Our baby should just about finish us off in our bedroom. We have absolutely no room. We all need our own places, but business first." Leon was rambling on and on.

"You have so much ambition and drive, Leon, I'm proud of you. Of course, I wish you mazel [good luck] in whatever you do. I only want the best for all of us." Excusing herself, Zelda said she must go and lie down for half an hour if Leon could keep an eye on Sol, as he just exhausted her. "I just have no energy right now."

After resting for a while, she felt a little more relaxed. She lay there, thinking of the significance of what Leon had said. He was a good husband, and she knew if and when he made a decision to quit his job, it would only be if he was certain they could all benefit from it.

Having made a thick barley soup with lots of potatoes and meat in it, which they could eat with bread and a nice salad, there was nothing to rush up for. Hannah was visiting their mother, who was still at Aunt Anna's, and Benjamin was meeting her there after his work. Zelda felt herself slip into a delightful light sleep.

Looking in on Zelda, Leon saw she was asleep, and deciding not to wake her, he gave Sol his bath, fed him, and then sat himself down on the floor, playing with him. When Zelda awoke to hear Sol's laughter, "More, Poppa," he was shouting. She came into the kitchen and laughed too. There was Leon lying across the floor, with his head peeping over the cupboard door, playing peekaboo.

"One more time, young man, and bed for you—I can see Poppa's fed you. Give Momma a kiss goodnight, and I'll come in and see you soon," Zelda told the child.

Leon raised him on his shoulders, shouting, "And off to bed we go, everyone mind, out of the way. Here we come." Sol thought all this was hilarious and clung to Leon's neck and said, "I'm not going to let you go, Poppa. You come to bed with me," with a pleading look in his eyes.

"Hurry up, Leon, dinner's ready," Zelda called out.

"You see, son, Poppa has to go eat now, so you be a good boy and go to sleep and we will play again tomorrow, God bless. Give Poppa a big hug, love you." Leon stood there, looking down at his son, who had become his everything.

A few hours later, Hannah and Benjamin came in, and they all sat around, talking about their forthcoming venture, the fact that one year would be the maximum they would all be able to live in this apartment. First, Zelda was due to have the baby in about a month, with Sol now nearly three years old, he was into everything and needed to be watched like a hawk. Hannah, on the other hand, was no more than three months pregnant but was already enormous, and everyone thought it was twins. There was a definite history of twins in Benjamin's family.

So it was decided that they must scrimp and save in order to buy a little stock for their cart. "We will not need much to start with, and we can build it up as we go along." Leon had been watching the other traders. As they sold, they replenished.

"But what shall we sell, and how much shall we charge?" Hannah asked, looking at Benjamin.

"We know, we know. You leave it to us. We will not have you worry your pretty heads. You will have enough to think about with the new babies," Benjamin told her as he just could not stand his beautiful Hannah to have any worry at all, and so it was with Leon. Although neither one could give great luxury to their wives, it was them that were the providers. As meager as the creature comforts were at this time, they had high hopes of bringing them up to greater levels.

They worked hard for the other traders, pulling their carts around from place to place, but it was not a bad job as at the end of the day, they could have their pick of the fruit and vegetables that had not been sold in the past few days and were just on the turn. They managed to get enough supply for themselves and Uncle Dov, for which Aunt Anna was always very grateful, and as their mother-in-law, Zena, was still staying with Dov and Anna, they felt this was the least they could do.

Occasionally when one of the traders had a good day, they gave them an extra few centimes, and gradually, they built up their reserves. Zelda gave birth to a daughter and called her Esther after Leon's grandmother, and as she held the baby one night to her breast, in came Leon and so their conversation began.

"Hello there, gorgeous girls, how are you getting on tonight?"

"I really do not know if she is getting enough milk. It is a great worry not knowing what she is taking. She is so tiny and solely reliant on me. When she cries, I just give it to her again, and now I am getting sore already. How do I know?"

"What are you worried about? Relax, for goodness' sake. You can see she is getting on. Look how her little cheeks are filling out. I'd take her from you and wind her, but my hands are so frozen stiff that I need at least an hour to thaw out." It was midwinter, freezing cold outside, and as he was talking to her, he started peeling off layers of outer clothing.

Sol had been taken over to Booba (Grandmother) Zena so that Zelda could try to get into a regular schedule with the baby, and of course, she always had a willing helper in Hannah, who was definitely having twins from the look of her, getting so big Zelda made fun of her, saying, "You are walking now like a duck," but also watching carefully as she saw her get breathless very easily.

Leon went into the kitchen. "Any room for me in here?" he jokingly asked his sister-in-law. "I certainly could do with something hot to warm me through." Hannah had made a big pot of chicken soup, loads of carrots, pieces of chicken cut up in it, giblets, and had even made kneidlach (similar to dumplings) and willingly gave him a full plate.

"How are things going, Leon? It is so hard for you in this snowy and icy weather, pulling those heavy carts around. It is so slippery out that I am not taking any chances of falling at this stage of my pregnancy, and anyway, I am pleased to have an excuse that I have a lovely new niece to help to look after."

"Well, I will tell you that it gets so cold out there that I cannot feel my fingers and toes, and now from the warmth in here, I feel like I am on fire." He pulled off another sweater very hurriedly. He now remained in a vest and pants whilst he hurriedly spooned in the soup as he had not eaten all day, and waves of hunger were now being satisfied.

"Your face has gone very red, like a beetroot." Hannah started laughing.

"That is what I like about you, Hannah. You can always find time to have a laugh and a joke." Leon bent over and gave his sister-in-law an affectionate peck on the cheek.

There was a loud knocking on the door. Leon went to answer it and seemed very quiet out there for about five minutes, so Hannah looked around the kitchen door and called, "Leon, is anything the matter?" Ashen-faced, Leon came back in with the sad news Uncle Judah had just passed away. The funeral was to be in the morning, as with Jewish tradition it was usually the very next day.

Dov was there standing behind Leon, and as Hannah saw him, she put her arms out to her uncle. A quietness came over them all, as Dov remembered other members of his family that had already passed on. Hannah could not help but think how old and gray her dear uncle looked and sadly began to wonder how long they would have him with them.

"Is something wrong with Momma? I thought I heard you, Uncle Dov. Is she ill? What is the matter?" As she was speaking, Zelda was looking from one to another, still holding baby Esther in her arms, that by the time she had asked the question, she felt her whole world was about to collapse around her. She grasped hold of the door and fumbled for a chair. Leon rushed to her side and told her of the sad news of Uncle Judah. Zelda burst into tears, and Leon took the baby from her. "I am so sorry for Aunt Anna, but God forgive me I thought it was my momma."

Dov left soon after. As the burial arrangements had already been made, there was no help they could offer. Benjamin came in soon after, and looking around at the sad faces, he was quickly informed as to what had happened.

"He was so good," Hannah said. "He would never hurt a fly and worked so hard on that farm. His only joy was to bring over a sack of potatoes now and then to his sister so that he thought he was helping in some way, feeling her family was his family."

"I guess he was a little simple in a nice way," Leon said. "After his wife died in childbirth, he never ever remarried, although Uncle Dov did try to introduce him to quite a lot of women. But he did not want anyone, God rest his soul."

"How do you know these things? Did he ever discuss this with you? I feel so sorry for Aunt Anna. After all, he was the only one from her side that ever bothered with her, and now he has gone." Zelda, feeling much calmer, could only think of wonderful things he had said and done, and secretly thought that she was lucky to have been spared her mother for whatever time there was left to them all. She loved her dearly.

The day was overcast and gray, and as the men made their way back from the burial grounds, each with their own private thoughts, it was doubly sad to think that Anna had the lone shiva (mourning) chair. On their return, Anna, who had not gone to the grounds, lit the candles together with the Yahrzeit (remembrance) light. As they came in, they washed their hands upon entering, which was the custom after a burial; the basin of water had been placed by the door. And so the week of shiva began.

The shiva week was long and drawn out. At night, there were so many people there for the minyan (prayers) that many were standing outside in the freezing cold as the apartment was too small to accommodate everyone. Benjamin and Leon came every night for the services and then went home for their evening meal. Both Zelda and Hannah came in the morning to sit with their aunt and see their mother, leaving only to take care of Sol and Esther. Hannah was finding great difficulty these days and had to be off her feet a lot because of swelling. Cooking their evening meal actually before they went out in the morning, they made extra food so they could take it to the shiva house each day.

Dov drew Benjamin and Leon to one side and said, "You are like my own children, to see you both married to my nieces and see how much you have tried since you have been here. You are working so hard to better yourselves, and slowly and surely, things are taking shape for you. Judah did not have much but the few francs he was saving for his old age . . . Ugh," he said, choking up. "No one takes it with them. Anna and I would like you both to have it to start yourselves in your new venture. It is not much, but we know this would have made Judah happy."

Screaming out in pain, Hannah had awoken in the night, with her bed saturated with water. Zelda rushed in. "What is going on? Are you all right?" As she arrived, Benjamin was running out the door to get some help.

"No, I do not know what is going on. Please get Momma, please get someone to help me." Zelda was lying there, moaning.

"Please don't worry, little one. This is all part and parcel of having a baby. You will be perfectly fine, and I am here with you always. Come, let me help you get up, and I will get a clean sheet. Let us change out of those wet clothes and make you comfortable."

With that, Hannah said, "Everything is hurting. I have low niggling pains and the most terrible backache."

"It is fine, it is fine, all perfectly normal. Just think positive thoughts that at the end of this, you will have not one but two beautiful babies. I cannot wait until I have my own nieces or nephews. How lucky you are to have two together." Zelda was carrying on this conversation to keep her focused and not scared. She remembered how very scared she was when Sol was born and with such pain she thought she was dying, and yet as soon as he had arrived, the feeling of elation was overwhelming. Of course, when Esther was born, she knew what to expect, and now she could not imagine her life without her beautiful children.

Zelda busied herself with a clean sheet, but before she put it down, she laid sheets of paper under it to protect the mattress. The sheet did not matter. They had got some really old sheets from Aunt Anna a few weeks ago, so they would bundle the lot up and throw them away once the birth was over. She put some water on to boil and asked her sister if she could get her anything and sat back, not knowing what else she could do. She felt so helpless hearing Hannah moaning softly.

In walked Momma with Aunt Anna, and they took over completely. Aunt Anna said, "We have called Mrs. Finkelstein, and she will be around soon. She is the one that has been doing all the births lately, so we will be here to assist her. How are you feeling, my lovely niece? Here, hold my hand," Zelda said. "You have not had some pain for a while, so perhaps you could get up and just walk up and down. It will help. Come along now, Hannah, just for a little bit to keep things moving."

Hours went by. Mrs. Finkelstein came, felt all around Hannah's stomach, and then said, "Raise your legs," and very quickly inserted two fingers into her vagina and declared, "She is nowhere near ready yet. Baby, or in this case, babies will not be born until they are good and ready. Let us all have a cup of tea." Everyone laughed and tried to relax.

Zena never left her side. They had all left the room and went out on the landing when Benjamin popped his head around the door. "Are you all right, sweetheart?"

Zena shouted out at him, "Away with you, this is no place for a man."

"Momma, please tell him I am all right. He must be so anxious." Hannah was clutching her mother's arm. "Please, Momma."

So Zena shouted to Benjamin, "It will be soon. She is well."

About another hour went by. Hannah was in strong labor now, and Mrs. Finkelstein had turned her on her side, telling her to push down hard. "Push, push, take some deep breaths, and when you feel the pain come again, push hard, my lovely. Push, push. Here is the baby's head. Push. Yes, he is crying. Yes, let us wrap him up. You have a beautiful son." Everyone in the room was crying, and about ten minutes went by and Hannah started screaming and pushing all over again. The afterbirth came out whole with no trouble, right after which her baby daughter was born so quickly that no one had a chance to even think about it. They were busy washing her and wrapping her.

Once the afterbirth came away, they cleaned her up quickly. Hannah sat like a queen, pillows all propped up behind her and with a baby in each arm. She was smiling but with tears of joy running down her face as Benjamin walked in and proudly looked at her and bent over to kiss her. "Thank you, my darling, I cannot believe that we are the parents of a boy and a girl. What an achievement. What else can I say but I, Benjamin, am at a complete loss for words because I feel that I am to my brim of happiness and we have waited for this day for so long that I must be dreaming."

Harry had his circumcision whilst the family gathered round, celebrating whilst baby Ada lay in Hannah's arms. Zena sat next to her, comforting her as she was crying. "Do not worry. Two seconds it takes, and he will be perfect." For health reasons and as was the custom, all Jewish males were circumcised eight days after being born.

The weather had turned beautiful. It was now at the end of April still a little brisk but if one kept a jacket or sweater handy it was delightful to walk, so the two Sisters with their little ones decided to pack a lunch and head toward the Seine. Vendors were out hawking their wares. Zelda and Hannah had no extra money for baubles but saw no harm in looking anyway.

They each pushed their prams. Esther was nicely bundled up and lay fast asleep. Harry and Ada, being still so small, were able to share the same pram. Harry was asleep, but Ada was looking up at the sky and looked like she would doze off any second. Little Sol was feeding the pigeons as they walked and was having such a good time, running a little ahead then stopping and trying to talk to them as he fed them some bread.

Leon and Benjamin had been quarreling so much lately that the sisters both decided they would keep well out of it. They told their individual husbands that whatever went on at work, please do not bring arguments back home with them. Leon however was continually walking around in a mood, slamming doors and scraping chairs, whereas Benjamin was quiet and never mentioned anything to Hannah. "Please, Leon, enough is enough. What has got into you? You were so happy with Benjamin and going into business together, but now you are forever in a temper." Zelda was beside herself with this aggravation. All Leon said was "He is such a shmuck" (fool, stupid).

The brothers-in-law argued constantly over several months when one night Benjamin came home. "Darling Hannah, we have to talk I really cannot work with Leon anymore. I cannot live in the same house walking out whenever he walks in, working with him and never discussing how things should be. He makes all the decisions and ignores me, I want the best for my family, so now I am asking you to leave all this behind us and let us go to America. I have some family there, and if I can work hard here, I can do it anywhere."

"My family though is here, Benjamin. What would Mother say?"

"Your mother would only want the best for us. We are your family, Hannah. Our children Harry and Ada come with us, my love, wherever we would be. I know you would miss Momma. We could always send for her. Or if not, I will go first and then send for you once I have a place and settled."

Zelda started crying, "How can you do this, Hannah?" when she told her. "We have always been together. I cannot bear to think you would be so far away and the children not being able to grow up together. What about Momma?"

Sobbing, Hannah took hold of her sister, hugged her, and said, "We will always be together. You will come visit me and I, you. We must not worry about Momma. She would only want our happiness. She can come live with you and then perhaps me—her choice. But she will always have a home with either one of us. Benjamin said he will go as soon as he finds out some more details about the trip, and he said Leon can have whatever business they have built up. He does not want anything at all. Do not fret, my precious sister, we will not be going for a long time. Benjamin will go first, and before we join him, he will get settled with a job and a place for us to live."

During his daily work, Benjamin started talking to everyone he could about immigrating to America. Everyone had a different idea of how to go about things, but a few people spoke to him of their relatives and what they had done. It was not easy, but what in life was? He was told by quite a few to go to Calais, get any ship he could across the Channel to England, and then make his way up to Glasgow. Apparently, all the big ships sailed from there, and because of the dangerous large expanse of water, there had been many shipwrecks. The year was 1887.

Benjamin decided he would save a little more money and leave in one month's time. This was an extremely hard time in their marriage, but feeling remorseful, he held her tight every night and listened to her as she wept. "I love you, my darling. You will see. This will be good for us all."

Time flew by, the month seemed to come so quickly, and as Hannah clung to him in the doorway, he said, "Look after Harry and Ada." With that, he was gone. Hannah sat herself down on a chair, and Zelda put her arm around her to comfort her.

When he eventually arrived at the docks in Calais, he asked where the booking office was. Speaking fluent French by this time, he felt confident as to what he was doing. However, to his bewilderment, there was a very long line waiting. Finally, it was his turn. "I want to travel to England."

"Next week" was the reply, and with that, the ticket master closed his shutter. Overhearing the conversation, the man in front of him turned around and said, "If you have money, there is no problem. I was here yesterday and now I have a ticket, so go find a place to sleep tonight and come back first thing in the morning. You will be able to book something."

The next day, Benjamin arrived at the ticket office very early, and when finally it was his turn, he said, "I want to pay as a passenger to sail to Glasgow."

Looking through his files, the ticket master replied, "I may be able to fit you in next Monday with your own cabin. It will be expensive though." By this time, Benjamin was not taking any chances and so he slipped him a few francs extra for himself, the ticket master grunted and handed him his ticket. Satisfied he took himself back to the boarding house where he had spent the previous night and booked himself through until the following Monday.

Upon arrival in Glasgow, he found the fare to America so high he enquired if any hands were needed on board. Finding out a vacancy had just been posted, he pretended to have had previous experience and made up some names of captains that could give references. The *State of Georgia* was both a cargo and passenger ship and would be pulling out in two weeks to the port of New York. Rough seas and cramped conditions below, he was throwing up violently sick, and he really had no idea just how hard the work was. Somehow, he managed. The journey was only twelve days, so each day was one day less.

Language was the main problem. The captain spoke German, so that made life a little easier as Yiddish and German were very similar; however, to his dismay, he soon found out that there was anti-Semitism on board. Everyone was all right to him except the head steward. Every time the toughest jobs needed to be done, he pointed in his direction shouting out, "Jude." Benjamin did not say a word and got on with whatever work needed to be done, thinking, "You bastard," but did not express any emotion, which aggravated the steward more.

Miraculously, so he thought, he arrived in New York. He got off the ship with a sigh of relief and with his wages tucked in a special belt Hannah had made him around his waist, which was not visible as it was under his trousers, he took his first step onto American soil. There was deep snow and slush everywhere as the sun came out and the snow was melting a little. Looking around, he felt his whole body shudder, and for the first time, he felt nervous. "Oy vey [oh my goodness], what have I done?" he was muttering to himself. Arriving in this big country, not speaking the language and with not much money, he carried the address of his cousin, but he had no idea which way to go. His thoughts centered on his beautiful Hannah and their baby twins.

Wandering on, he found a policeman and showed him the paper with the address, and he pointed in the direction he needed to go, so he walked and walked, carrying his small case and his bag, which was virtually all his belongings. After stopping several people who were rushing by, he tried to talk to them. They did not understand him or he they, which he found so frustrating. Determinedly, he thought, "I will conquer this language as I did French, no way am I an idiot," as he plodded on.

Finally, he saw a shop that was a Jewish deli. He went inside, and the smells made him realize how absolutely famished he was and, in Yiddish, asked to eat. The owner came right over to him and showed him a seat and sat alongside him and asked him, "Veir kimmen du? Veir Gaist du?" (Where have you come from? Where are you going?)

What a stroke of luck, Benjamin thought, as he started to eat and speak at the same time. He shoveled the food into his mouth as he apologized to the owner, saying, "Please excuse me. I did not realize how hungry I was." He then introduced himself as Benjamin and told him of his journey to America and that he had only just arrived. He had left his family in France and had come hoping to meet up with his cousin.

"My name is Joseph. Here in America, everyone shortens or changes their names, so they call me Joe. You I shall call Ben. Where did you originally come from before France?" So their friendship began. Joe too had come from Russia and, it turned out, from a shtetl not far from where Benjamin's family were from.

"I must write to my wife to let her know I arrived safe. We have two beautiful baby twins, and once I get myself settled, I will send for them as soon as I can."

"Yetta, come meet Ben, from the haim [homeland], just arrived." Joe's wife, a rather zaftig (full-figured) woman, came from behind the counter, wiping her hands on her apron. She had a warm smile and greeted Benjamin with a hug and welcomed him to their deli. "Everyone seems to make their way here. Our food is becoming famous." She laughed.

"I was thinking, Yetta, Ben does not know the language and has nowhere to stay at the moment. We could use a little help. Maybe he could stay with us for a little while until he feels comfortable in the big city. New York can make you feel overpowered."

So it was agreed by all. Several days turned into several months. Delancey Street became his home. He helped during the day and tried so hard to conquer the language at night. Sophie, their twelve-year-old daughter, was sitting with him, saying the words, and he was repeating them after her. It was at first seemingly impossible to learn this language, but then all of a sudden, it all began to click in his head and it seemed he was trying to hold a conversation.

Feeling more confident, he told them, "I am so grateful to all of you. I do not know how I could ever repay you for your kind generosity to me, a complete stranger, but it is time for me to move on and try to find my cousin. This is why I came to America." Gathering around him, they said it was their pleasure and please keep in touch with them and let them know how things turn out.

Walking around New York was very exciting. It was a hustle and bustle, with people everywhere, vendors on the street corners, trying to make a dollar. Benjamin could not get over the clothes people were wearing. They were so very colorful. Everyone seemed to have hats, women with the most ornate ones, men with trilbies or caps. He himself was wearing an old cap and swore to himself that he too would buy himself some new clothes as soon as he was able.

Trudging along, he reached his cousin's address on Eighty-seventh Street, a tenement-style block of apartments. Nervously, he went and knocked on the door of #8 Chisholm Buildings; however, no one answered. David must be at work, he thought, so taking his case and his bag along with him, he went to a local café and asked for a lemon tea to while away the time.

"Hi, are you going somewhere nice?" the waitress asked.

"Thank you, but I have arrived from France and I am going to see my cousin David Markovich. He lives here, but at the moment, he is not home and must be at work. Do you know him?" Benjamin said in his broken English.

"No, I have never met him. Did he know you were coming? What's your name? My name is Alice Brown." Beautiful she was not, pretty, yes, in a very alluring way with such a warm personality that Benjamin fell immediately under her charm.

"My name is Benjamin, but now they call me Ben. I wrote to him from France, outlining my intention of coming to America, as years ago he had told me that anytime I wanted to come, I would always have a roof over my head with him. I should have written him actually when I arrived, but I have been staying with a family on the Lower East Side and trying to learn a little to speak in American."

Alice laughed and laughed at his gorgeous accent, eying his broad physique and thinking to herself that he was quite a hunk and also thinking that she wanted to get to know him better.

"Well, Ben, you can stay here as long as you like. It is only 4:30 p.m. and if your cousin is working, he may be hours yet. I tell you what, at 6:00 p.m., go check again, or if you want to have a walk around, you can always leave your things here. I will put them behind the counter for you. I do not get off until ten every evening, so I hope that we can be friends and you will feel you can always come in and talk anytime."

So another friendship was formed, but this girl with her carefree way and laughter made him forget all the hardship he had in his life and, for a few moments, even forget his life in Paris. "Thank you so much, Alice, you are so kind. Yes, I will go out and have a walk around for an hour or so and then come back soon if that is all right with you. I would like to see the neighborhood."

Leaving his case and bag behind the counter as Alice had suggested, he wandered out and was so fascinated that he stood for an hour on the corner of Eighty-eighth Street, where three men were playing music: one a fiddle, the other drums, and one a trumpet. He had never heard such sounds, but he was loving it. People were stopping by and throwing a cent or two into a hat. They were so terrific people started dancing as they were walking by. He thought, "I wonder if they are famous. If they are not, I am sure one day they will be."

Wandering back, he thought he would try his cousin's apartment first, and then if he was not in, he would go back to the café and write him a note and leave it under his door. His thoughts were miles away. So much to think about, mostly the new language he really had to concentrate so hard on anything that was being spoken, but he was making progress each day and feeling full of confidence, he knocked again on David's door. No answer. "Oh well," he muttered out loud and headed back to the café.

"What's going on? Did you see anything interesting? There is always something happening here in New York. I forgot to tell you though to be careful of pickpockets. Plenty of them around, and plenty of con men that would talk you into anything and then rob you blind."

"I went to watch a group playing instruments on the next street on the corner. They were terrific. People were dancing and they had a hat, which some threw money into. I have never heard that type of music before, and I was truly fascinated with it. Then I walked back to David's apartment, but he was still not in. Alice, do you have some paper and a pencil? I will write him a note that I am here and leave it under his door."

"Yes, sure." Tearing a piece of paper off of her checkbook and handing him her pencil, she said, "Tell him to meet you here. That is the best thing. Then you don't have to keep going back."

Benjamin scribbled the note, rushed back to the apartment, and pushed it under the door. After going back to Alice, he said, "I never thought about the fact he may not be home. I guess in my mind, he would be waiting for me and know I was coming. How stupid of me. I do not know what I shall do if he is not there, or maybe he does not live there anymore."

"Please don't worry, honey. It will all work out in the end. You will see." With that, she poured him a bowl of soup and gave it to him with a big hunk of bread. Looking at him and really feeling sorry for him, she said, "You must be starving. You will think and feel much better on a full stomach. When did you last eat?"

"How kind, Alice, I have not had anything since early this morning when I had a bagel. Maybe I should head back to Delancey Street and write to him and wait until he answers me, meshuggener kop. Sorry, you do not know this, but I am saying that I have a mad head, that I was not thinking ahead because I was so concentrating on working at the delicatessen and trying to learn a little American."

"You mean English, Ben. Americans speak English. Anyway, I am not being forward, but I leave work at 10:00 p.m., and if you cannot reach your cousin by then, I will put you up until morning."

"Would you really do that for me, Alice, a complete stranger? I cannot believe how kind everyone has been to me in America."

"Do not be fooled. Not everyone is kind, and most would roll you over for every nickel that you would have. I hope things work out for you with your cousin. You have come an awful long way and have left all your family behind, because you just want the best for them." Alice was looking at him and thinking to herself that he was so manly and she was so attracted to him, besides which, she couldn't believe that she had volunteered to put him up for the night.

Benjamin went to check if his cousin was there every hour on the hour; however, 10:00 p.m. came around, and Alice gathered her things and said, with a big smile, "Well, come on if you are coming. Otherwise, it is the street for you." Benjamin followed her out, carrying his case in one hand and his bag in the other. They headed to Ninety-fourth Street, where Alice had a one-room apartment. "I am not used to entertaining a man friend here. Toilet and washroom are just down the hall. Here's a towel and soap, and I will see you when you get back."

Alice turned down the bed, and when Benjamin came back, she said, "You will sleep on one half and I on the other."

"No, no, I really cannot do that."

"Why not? I am not going to attack you, and remember this is America. Do not worry. I am not, so why should you?"

Benjamin thought, "She is so kind, so pretty. I really like her."

Alice took her nightgown and went to wash up. When she came back, she got herself into bed. Getting very close to him, she said, "Ben, you must be very lonely. It is already such a long time since you have been with a woman. Come, I will not bite you, I promise. Just put your arms around me and touch me, take advantage of the moment."

Feeling himself harden and liking the feeling, he felt her hand go down under his pants. "Oh, what are you doing? You don't even know me. I am a married man with twins. I really should not be doing this." She kissed his neck and snuggled closer; her hand was working on his penis. He gave a groan and pulled her to him. "I cannot believe I am doing this," he said.

"Believe it, believe it," she said breathlessly. "Take off these clothes and let me treat you to something special." She was pulling at his clothes, whilst she took off her nightdress. Her tongue was licking him from his lips, down his chest, across his stomach, and down to his penis. When she finally reached him, she put him right into her mouth, turning so she was face down on him. Her legs were wide apart near his head. "Do the same for me. I will show you how sex should be."

Without thinking, Ben reached down and put his tongue in her vagina, holding on to her legs. He felt every bone in his body shaking and then with a shudder, he pulled her off him and twisted her body on to her back and entered her for a second before he came. "I could not hold it any longer, Alice. You have some body and you are some woman. I have never experienced sex like it. You are unbelievable. Is this true or is this a dream?"

"Then, my dearest Ben, we will be the best of friends and now lovers until you are reunited with your family. Do not worry. This goes on a lot here in America. As long as you enjoy my body, I am loving yours. Tomorrow, you can leave another note for your cousin to contact you at the café or this address, and you can stay here for as long as you want. I will be loving every minute of it, and of course you if you can stand it."

They both laughed, curled up in each other's arms, and fell asleep. In the morning, he was wide awake but lay there staring at her, her long hair sprawled all over his chest and he lay next to her without moving in case he disturbed her, but then he bent down and kissed her head gently, wondering how lucky he had been to meet this angel who had been unbelievably kind to him and then the sex. Never in a million years did he ever know about oral sex. Did anyone ever do it in the haim (homeland)? He doubted it, probably not kosher.

He was smiling to himself when she stirred and nestled into the curve of his body. Oh God, he felt his penis harden. He did not want it to, but it had a mind all of its own.

"Good morning, honey, I feel my man down there is also awake, so come on, give him some exercise, put him in me. My body is aching for you, and I am loving it." Ben, without any hesitation, eased himself into her. They were still on their sides but she felt wet and it went in very quickly.

"Hold me tight, squeeze me," she was yelling. "Make me come."

Ben just did not understand what she was talking about. He thought, "I will have to ask her later." In the meantime, they had moved, and he was now lying and she was sitting on top of him, riding him like a horse. He held and fondled her breasts, and when his fingers went down to her clitoris, she was screaming by that time. He found himself moaning and pulling her down on him now with both hands on her hips. Never feeling such ecstasy before, he just let his body drift into oblivion. After making love, they both lay there spent, not caring about the sheets being wet. She nestled back into him, and they both drifted off into a deep sleep.

Awaking to the smell of cooking, Benjamin stretched. "Mm, smells nice whatever it is."

"Go get washed up, and I will make something nice for you." Slipping into his trousers and taking the soap and towel with him, Ben hurried down the hall to the toilet and sink, started washing himself from head to toe as there was no bath there. He found himself singing and whistling. Someone started banging on the door. "What you doing in there? Hurry up, I have to go."

Ben came out. "Sorry, I did not know anyone was waiting," he said to the irate neighbor.

"Just remember next time, buddy. We all have to share this godforsaken hole. I need to take a dump."

Not knowing what he was talking about, Ben hurried back to the room, and seeing Alice there, he went over and pulled her to him. "Thank you for the most amazing night I have ever had, thank you for being such an amazing woman."

She threw back her hair, which was down nearly to waist length. "Ahh, come on now. You are a married man and you have children. This cannot be new for you. Come sit down and let us eat an American breakfast." She had made bacon and eggs. Not knowing what it was, he devoured it hungrily with the delicious bread Alice had brought back with her from the café last night.

"Mmm, good." Sitting back, sipping his coffee, he was looking at her in awe. "What was it I ate? I loved it. Obviously not kosher but something tells me not to even think about these things right now." They both laughed, and she said it was bacon he ate. Well, he said he would certainly be eating it again.

"Now last night I told you that you can stay here as long as you like. Why don't you go see if your cousin is home and leave him this address so this way you are not having to go back and forth. I have to be at work at 11:00 a.m. today. Here is the key and you can come in and out as you like. I hope you will come and sit in the café later tonight, then we can walk home together. I finish at 10:00 p.m." With that, she planted a kiss on his cheek and was gone before he could blink an eye.

Putting his head in his hands, trying to make sense of all this, feeling it was too overpowering, he felt his shoulders begin to shake, and tears ran down his face. His thoughts ran between his parents in Russia and his beautiful Hannah and gorgeous twins Harry and Ada. "What sort of example am I making for them?" he shouted out loud in his frustrated mind. "I had better write to Hannah just to let her know I am well, even though I do not have a forwarding address other than my cousin's. She will be so worried. I know her like a bad coin." Muttering to himself, he started looking round for some paper.

> My darling Hannah, so much is going on in this big city. I would like to start first of all by saying I am well and hope that you and our precious babies are the same. I still have not been able to contact David. I left him a note yesterday, so hopefully today we will be able to get together.
>
> My hopes are circled around him. My money will soon run out, so hopefully he may have something for me or recommend me. Once I get a job, I will feel so much better. I will write to you as soon as I can, hopefully with some better news on that subject. Not knowing which way to turn is the most terrible feeling, but have faith in me, my love. Believe

me, I know my responsibility is with you, Harry, and Ada, so I will be trying my very best. You know that.

I love you, dearest one. Stay strong, and I will write with better news in a few days.

Your adoring husband Benjamin

It was now already 1:00 p.m., and feeling mentally exhausted from the tension of having to sit down and write Hannah, feeling ashamed of what he had done, and facing up to these indiscretions, he lay down on the bed and fell into a mentally exhausted sleep. On awakening, he decided that he would enjoy the fruits of life that this relationship could offer him. After all, his wife and family need never know about it, and they would never suffer from whatever he was doing. "I guess this is part of living, part of survival as long as I do not hurt anyone by this, so I am going to carry on." He was now talking to himself.

Going down the hallway, he went into the washroom. As he was in no hurry, he took his time and gave himself a good shave. Looking back into the mirror, he felt pleased with what he saw and decided beards were definitely not his style. Now feeling much better about himself and life in general, he dressed and set off to see Alice and get something to eat at the café, suddenly feeling absolutely famished.

Looking around the café, which was really busy at 6:00 p.m., he did not see Alice at first, so he looked around for a vacant chair. "Do you mind if I join you?"

he asked a man and woman who seemed deep in conversation. The man motioned him to go away. There were no other seats available, so he went to stand by the counter. Alice came out from the back with two plates with sandwiches, which seemed enormous to Benjamin's growling stomach. He looked longingly at them.

"Hi there, sweetheart, can you hang out for a half an hour or so, by which time this place will have emptied out somewhat? Hey, I have a letter for you in the back, from your cousin. He will not be home until 9:00 p.m. I'll give it to you when you come back."

Reluctantly, Ben turned around and took a walk around to kill time. On one of the street corners, there was a guy that was selling roasted chestnuts. His oil drum was ablaze with coal, the heat from which absolutely radiated around him, and the aroma was unbelievable. The man had these little packets with hot nuts on a tray on top, just amazing. Ben stopped. "Yes, I would like one packet please, how much?"

"Two cents, thanks," he replied.

Paying this, Ben walked on with the warm packet in his hand. He enjoyed every mouthful. "I will buy them again another time," he thought, walking for about an hour and enjoying every minute of New York. The atmosphere, the people, just being here in general sent a thrill through him that he could not try to describe, deciding it was time to head back to the café, by which time hopefully it would not be so busy.

"Hi, honey," she called to him as he entered. "Sit down over there by the window. I am making you a sandwich, and I will be right with you." After a couple of minutes, out she came with a tray of soup and a sandwich piled high with turkey, lettuce, and tomato and potato chips all around it.

"Wow, that looks like some sandwich there, Alice, thank you."

"Made with my own little hands, but have your soup first. We make it fresh each day, and that will warm the cockles of your heart." Propped up beside the plate was an envelope with the message from his cousin. He was too hungry to read it at first, so he just ate like he had never seen food before.

Alice was busy with some customers. She had told her boss that this was the new man in her life, and he had squared it away with her that when he came in, she was not to charge him. He valued her work, he had told her, so whatever made her happy created a good atmosphere to portray to anyone she served. When she finally had finished serving the last customer, she came and sat down next to him. "Wow, look at you. I will check out how smooth you are later on. I love the look. All your stubble has gone, how handsome you look." Absolutely amazed, Benjamin had never ever been told he was handsome, and here he was feeling like he couldn't wait to get into bed with her again.

"Tell me, what does your cousin say?"

"Just very excited to know I am here, and that he would be home at 9:00 p.m. as he is working but will be home then, and that I am to come round at that time."

"Remember, honey, you do what you have to do. Maybe he can get you some work, but you can stay with me, no strings attached. I know you're married, but we can shack up together. But oh boy, we make happy music together."

They sat holding hands, with Alice jumping up every now and then to take care of a customer, and when Benjamin left to go to his cousin David, he promised he would be back at her apartment later on. "I cannot wait," she called out to him.

Walking to David's apartment, he could not help but wonder at this stroke of luck. As much as he loved Hannah, who was his whole life, he had never experienced anything quite as unbelievable as this. "Such words I am learning, she said she cannot wait to shack up with me again. She is amazing." Muttering away to himself, he reached his cousin's apartment.

Approaching the apartment, Benjamin with his heart clapping was so looking forward to seeing David but was nervous for his future. Would David be able to help him find a job? Would it be something he liked, would it be something he could use just as a stepping stone? Sure, he could stay with Alice. He had made up his mind that could definitely be the answer—of course, only until he could save and bring his family over. When that would be he had no idea, but first things first. He knocked on the door, apprehensive as to what David's greeting would be.

"Kim arien, kim, kim." (Come in, come, come.) David, a short stocky guy, threw his arms around Ben and gave him a massive bear hug. "When I found your note late last night, I was so excited. I cannot believe you are finally here, my dear cousin. Tell me first of all how you are, and what news do you have of the family back home?"

They spoke for a good hour about their respective families, and then David said that after getting his note yesterday, he had spoken to his boss. "Amazing, because he said to bring you in—he was actually thinking of hiring someone as an apprentice to learn the business, so he will interview you on Sunday. We are milliners, you know, people that make hats. Everyone, rich and poor, all wear hats, some very ornate, some plain, and we are very busy. It means, Benjamin, I mean, Ben, you would start from the bottom and learn the trade."

"That sounds very good. I will be a quick learner. How long do you think I would have to be an apprentice?"

"Well, when I started out with this company, I was an apprentice for a year. It is up to you because at the end of that time, you will be well in with the firm and then getting a living wage. First up though, you will only be getting a pittance, but you can stay with me for nothing. Ben, little is better than none, so I am very excited for you to try this. It is a nice, clean living, and once you know it, who knows how far you could go up the ladder?"

"Thank you so much, David, I am staying with a friend at the moment, but I might take you up on the accommodation later on. What time do we meet on Sunday?"

"Be here 7:00 a.m. We work a full day Sunday as we close early Friday and do not work Saturday. Come dressed like you are now. This is a factory, so no one comes in suit and tie. I think you will like it, I have been very happy there and now earn a good living."

"I hope so. I've taken this giant step by leaving my family behind me and trying to establish something for them to come to. It must be hard for Hannah with the twins without me. I am sorry, and I am not, because we had no life there. I had to get away from my domineering brother-in-law. We got ourselves into this position of not only living together but working together, and we were constantly arguing. Anyway, that is in the past. I gave Hannah your address to write me here."

"Oh my God, please forgive me in the excitement of seeing you and us talking—a letter came for you last week. Oh dear, I am sorry. Where did I put it? Hold on a minute!" Coming back into the room, he held up the letter. "Here it is, was by the side of my bed so I should not forget." They both laughed. Ben reached out his hand and thanked his cousin over again, bidding him good night and promising to be on time on Sunday. They parted at the door.

The cold air rushed around him as he walked rapidly to Alice. He had put the letter in his pocket and thought, "No, I've waited this long to hear from home, so I will not open this until tomorrow when Alice goes to work. I cannot read this and then make love to Alice." Thinking about the excitement of her body next to his, he hastened his step, not thinking and being aware of anyone around him when two burly guys came out of the shadows and demanded his money.

"I do not have any." He tried to sidestep them, but as he did, one took a punch at him whilst the other jumped him. Before he knew what was happening, he had been knocked to the ground whilst one of the men sat on his back, punching him and shouting, "Hand over your money," the other one rummaging through his pockets. He tried to struggle free but to no avail. They took off with fifty cents, which was all he had in his pockets. They ran off into the dark night. Ben got to his feet, sporting a black eye. "A mesa meshina [the worst curse] on you." He raised his fist in the air and shouted to no one as they had taken off like a bolt of lightning. He was thankful that his few dollars were safe in the belt Hannah had made for him, which was inside his trousers, around his waist.

There had been no one around to witness this. It was now 11:00 p.m. He felt for the letter in his pocket. Thank goodness that was still there but now because this had happened to him, he walked in the street so he was aware of everything, front, sides, and back of him, swearing this would never happen again. When he reached Alice's apartment, he fumbled with the key. His eye was smarting, and water was trickling out of it. He couldn't quite see to put the key in the hole, so he knocked on the door.

"Who is it?"

"It is me—Ben."

"What on earth has happened to you? Quick, come in and let me put a cold towel on that eye. My oh my, you have a real shiner there, my love. Come sit down and tell me what happened. Walking around New York is not safe anymore. There is so much unemployment, and people like those that just accosted you never want to work, so they will steal anything and everything they can. That is why I told you also to beware of pickpockets and con artists. I will make you a nice hot drink."

They spoke for a while, Ben telling her about his cousin and the offer to apprentice in the millinery factory so he could learn the business. He did not mention the letter from Hannah in case she insisted on him reading it, but he did say that he would not be earning very much for the first year and that David had offered for him to stay there.

Alice put her arm around him. "Let us take one day at a time, my darling. Right now, I hope you are happy staying here with me. Go get yourself washed and ready for bed. I won't attack you tonight as you must be sore as hell, which is a shame, but we will just cuddle." They both laughed, and Ben took his towel and soap and went off to the washroom down the hall as she had already done with her ablutions before he had arrived. She got into bed and waited for him in anticipation. Bruises were starting to appear on his body where they had beaten him, and he got into bed very gingerly as his whole body was aching. "Don't move, darling, just lie on your back and let me make love to you. You just lie there and enjoy and take your mind off your nasty experience."

Taking hold of his penis, she started by licking him all around the rim. He lay there moaning with enjoyment as she first started rubbing him gently then a little more vigorously. "I cannot move myself. Otherwise, I would just get on top of you now."

"No. No, shh, don't say a word, just relax." She took him in her mouth; her tongue did all the work, up and down until he came.

"No, no, my God, you are something else. I never knew making love could be like this, so satisfying, thought it was just to relieve oneself and nothing more, but the feelings you put into this is mind-boggling. I apologize I came in your mouth. You did not let go, and it just came. I could not stop." They lay entwined and spent, and fell asleep without saying another word.

Next morning, Alice got up and put up the coffee and started making her usual breakfast, eggs and bacon, and served Ben with big chunks of bread heavily buttered. "You are so good to me, Alice. If I stay here with you, I want to contribute to the household budget. Let me see how much I will get and then we have to have a very serious talk about it."

Smiling, Alice came around the table and lifted his face and planted a kiss on his lips. "Yes, we will talk but not now. Do not spoil the moment."

"I am just curious, Alice. You know so much about me, but really, I know nothing about you. We make love and yet you do not seem to worry about becoming pregnant. Your attitude toward sex is happy and carefree unlike most women, who do not want to be touched in case they become pregnant."

With that, Alice burst into tears. Ben rushed to her side. "What have I said? I am sorry if I have upset you so. Please tell me, Alice, my love. I would not want to hurt you for the world. God bless you, these have been the best days in my life except, of course, being beaten up." They both laughed, and it relieved the tension in the air.

"Maybe we will talk about it someday but not now. I do not have to go to work until 3:00 p.m., so I am going to suggest I make a picnic lunch and let us get out of here and enjoy the day."

Delaying the reading of the letter he had received from Hannah until Alice went to work, he sat down quietly and opened it:

> My darling Benjamin,
>
> How I miss you so very much is indescribable, I hope this finds you well as TG it leaves all of us here. Our beautiful twins are starting to get into everything, but they are so adorable I love them to pieces. Unfortunately,

I was not feeling the best after you left. I discovered I was pregnant, extremely sick but I am pleased to say that has passed. Yes, my darling husband, you will be a father again. No one believes it will be twins again. I hope not! I was not at all pleased at first with you so far away, and goodness knows when we will get together again but now I have adjusted my whole mind to another baby.

I do not want to burden you at all. Just do your best, and one day, we will all be together again.

I love you,
Hannah

Ben's days and nights at the factory were long and very tiring; he worked from 7:00 a.m. until 8:00 p.m., a thirteen-hour day, for which he earned $3 a week. He started every morning sweeping the floors and then running errands between the cloth manufacturers and picking up cotton or trimmings, which could be artificial flowers or beads or even little animals that were sewn onto the hats, the most amazing styles. He learned how to make the patterns, cut the material, sew by hand and machine, and most of all, block the hats onto the stands and work from that. When they were done, each one was put carefully into an individual box and labeled where it was destined to go. He learned that he had a dozen samples to work from, which had been shown and sold to the various stores. He also learned that there was much money to be made from this.

As Ben progressed in the company, the boss felt more and more confident in him and gave him more responsibilities. One day, he approached him saying, "My agent is ill, so tomorrow, I want you to put a suit on and go to where we are having a fashion show and take all the samples with you. I want you to take orders on them. Do you think you can do that?"

Once before, he had been an assistant at one of these shows but never left on his own. "Yes, of course I can," he said a little nervously.

"Get some nice orders for me, my boy, and there will be a raise for you in your pay packet."

On arrival back at Alice's café, he excitedly told her of the happenings of the day. "Wow, honey, you have made some impression on your boss to give you such responsibility. Here, I have made you some pea soup today, and a nice sandwich. You must be so hungry." Giving a little chuckle as she passed by him, she bent and whispered, "I hope you are hungry for me later on."

As they walked back to the apartment at 10:00 p.m. hand in hand, Ben put his arms around Alice and gave her a long lingering kiss in the street. "My oh my, boyo, you are something else tonight, hot stuff!"

"When we get back to the apartment, I just need to talk." As they approached and she put the key in the door, he took her in his arms again. They came in, and she immediately put on the kettle and said, "Come sit down and we will talk."

"Alice, you are on my mind night and day. Our relationship these last six months has been incredible, and I never thought for one previous moment of my life I would ever be disloyal to my family. I love you, Alice, and I will never give you up. Can you live with the knowledge that I am married with a family and will never divorce my wife? Help me, Alice, tell me what to do. I am telling you I love you but I love my family. Do you want me out of your life or do you want me in it? Help me. I have twins and now another on the way. I will never turn my back on them."

"I love you too, honeybun. I told you from the beginning that the fact you are married will never interfere with us. In the meantime, your wife is in Paris and you are here needing loving, and that is what I am prepared to do. You are saving little by little, and eventually, I know the family will come over. I told you, let us take one day at a time."

"A leiben on the keppalah [a blessing on your head]. I have asked you before though, and truthfully, I think about it often. Are you never worried about falling pregnant?" Alice started crying, and Ben put his arms around her immediately.

"I really did not want to talk about it because it brings back such terrible memories. However, you touched on this subject once before, I know, and I could never speak out about my past, but I feel now is the time to be open with you. No one, no one have I ever spoken to about this. I had an abusive father, and since I was eight, he used to do all sorts of things with me. He used to wake me out of my sleep, picking me up and carrying me into his bed, and he made it like play at first with a teddy bear. Touching me, he used to whisper in my ear to come hold and lick his cuddle teddy so he could go to sleep. I used to pray every night he would not come for me. Can you believe my mother turned a blind eye to it and said I was making it up? She was always pissed out of her mind and unaware of anything.

"At the age of twelve, I became pregnant, and my mother could no longer deny what a bastard her husband was. She took me to have an abortion. After I recovered, I ran away. I have never been in touch with them since. I made up my mind he would never touch me again. It has been hard for me, Ben, and yes, I lived with a guy for a while who was kind at first, but I have worked and strived to put this little lot together. I have enjoyed sex in the past but have not wanted any commitments. That is why I say let us take one day at a time.

"Pregnancy, I do not think so. They probably butchered me up, but if a baby came, I would sure love it and protect it."

"I am so sorry, darling Alice. I had no idea, and I promise I will never talk about it again now I understand. Come, let us go to bed, but to sleep. I did not realize the time we have been talking for so long, and I had a heavy day. I have to be in the factory promptly at 7:00

a.m. to take the samples to the store that is having its grand opening tomorrow. It is a company called B. Altman on Fifth. We have reserved a room there, so we hope to take orders and ship our hats wherever we can. Apparently, my boss is a real go-getter, and anywhere he can, he goes after those orders."

The day went very successfully. He arrived at the factory promptly at 7:00 a.m. with an air of enthusiasm. Mr. Katz was waiting for him, strutting back and forth with a cigar in his mouth. "Now listen here, young man, I am entrusting you with a very important job. This collection of hats is worth a lot of money," he emphasized. "Do not let them out of your sight, do you hear me?"

"Yes, Mr. Katz, I am looking forward to the day, and I will do the very best for you." Ben's command of the English language had so improved that it made him feel confident to tackle anything.

"Now, first of all, we will load the boxes up on the trolley, and you will wheel it through until you come to Altman's on Fifth. When you arrive, ask where the fashion show will be for millinery. There will be a long table allocated for you. It should have our name on it: Katz's Millinery. Place the dummy heads on it and take each hat out of the box and make sure they appear beautiful from the front, fluff them up, you know, how I have shown you. Here are the order forms. You look nice, Ben, I am pleased to say. Write clearly with name and address.

"All the hats have a style number on the tag and price, also what colors are available in that style. I will personally come over to see how you are getting on later in the day. I cannot stay because I have to be in the factory, but that can give you a toilet break.

"Good luck, young man, I have a lot of faith in you."

Setting off down Seventh Avenue, pushing the cart in front of him so that he could keep an eye on the boxes rather than pulling it behind him and maybe losing one en route, he cut across Thirty-fourth Street to Fifth, and on arrival at the store, he asked where the fashion show would be today and excitedly proceeded to set up his beautiful samples. There were other designers there already setting up models with dresses and coats, but he noted there were no others with hats. "Good," he told himself. His stomach was churning as this was his big chance.

People started coming into the room slowly around 9:00 a.m., and Ben, putting on his full charm, managed to take an order or two. He was rather disappointed, but by noon, he had taken quite a few. In fact, one store out West had ordered a dozen from him. When Mr. Katz came around at 1:00 p.m. to relieve him so he could go to the bathroom and grab a quick bite, he said, "Well, my boy, I have found a gem in you. Continue to work hard for me, and you will reap the rewards."

When the store was closing, Ben put the hats back in the boxes together with the blocks and proceeded back to the factory with everything intact, including his order book, and was overjoyed at Mr. Katz's reaction. "Oh my God in heaven, did you twist people's arms? Fantastic achievement to bring in orders from across the country, six dozen altogether. Tomorrow we will get busy making and finishing them. This is the start, my boy chick. You will start making good money now and soon be able to bring your family over. David tells me you have a new baby son, mazel tov. Let us start by giving you a pay raise to double what you was getting before. Now it will be $6 a week, and I will also put you on a commission basis. Whenever you go out to sell, you will get an additional $1 a dozen."

With his reputation, Ben's life became a whirlwind of appointments. Eventually, Mr. Katz decided he would open a showroom and put Ben solely in charge of it, the most beautiful and ornate millinery becoming a household word. If you had a Katz hat, it was to be envied by all.

Money became his main object now, with his orders, his commission plus his base salary was the most important thing to him. He made up his mind he would buy a house in Lakewood, New Jersey, when he had saved enough, then he would be able to bring Hannah and the children over as there was a very nice Jewish community there for them to grow up in. He would then be able to commute each week to the city and be able to stay with Alice during that time but then go back on weekends to his family, enjoying the best of two worlds.

France was hustling and bustling. Leon had now developed his business so much that he had opened a shop right in the middle of Paris near the Champs-Élysées and attracted many wealthy clients, working his way up from selling cheap clothing in the market. Many now came to him for his exclusive designs. Working well with a cutter and pattern maker between them, they were coming up with the most different and unusual dress designs, exactly what the upper classes wanted. Money was no problem these days. He worked hard, sometimes well into the night, with drawing pads in front of him.

They had moved their apartment several times for larger accommodation, but today, Leon came home and said to Zelda, "Come with me. We need to go somewhere. Leave the baby with Hannah, just get ready quickly. I will wait for you." Their new son had been named David after Uncle Dov, who had passed away last year.

Once again, Leon was feeling cramped and needed space. He still had his darling sister-in-law Hannah and her three children living with them. Leon basically kept them, although Benjamin did send small amounts of money to Hannah. Feeling so very angry, he would not say so to Zelda. He had the feeling his brother-in-law the serator (nutcase) had abandoned them to his charity as it was now twenty-five years since he had gone, and good riddance to him.

Breaking his chain of thought, out of the bedroom came his beautiful wife. "I'm all made up and ready to go, where to I don't know." Taking his arm, she called out to Hannah, "Thank you, do not know where he is taking me. Baby has been fed, but if I am not back by five o'clock, please feed the children."

They had now five children, although this last baby had taken them all by surprise. David had arrived ten years after his sister Becky. Zelda had thought she was finished with childbirth, but he was certainly a blessing. Their oldest, Sol, had married a very beautiful girl, who was pregnant with their second baby, and Leon had taken him into the business so he could expand and spread their wings out of Paris. He was told there was plenty of business to be had in the South of France, so they were both going there next week to look for a suitable location to open a second branch.

It was a lovely summer day. Zelda, dressed in a lime-green outfit with a matching hat, looked stunning. They made small talk about the children, all the time heading toward the Seine. Looking around, Zelda said, "Where are we going? Did you just want to get out of the shop and get some fresh air, because it truly is a magnificent day, and believe me, I have no objection. It is a tonic for me to get out lately."

"Just enjoy the sunshine, Zelda, be patient. We will soon be there."

"You are impossible. Never do you tell me anything but want to surprise me, and you do not realize how frustrated that makes me," Zelda said angrily. "Well, we are here now. Tell me if you are still frustrated with me, my darling. You know I only want the best for you and our lovely family."

Leon was feeling very proud of himself as they reached the block of apartments overlooking the Seine. Looking up toward the top, he said, "Come, my love, see for yourself how magnificent this is. This is my dream come true."

Opening the door to apartment 21, Zelda stood there in the doorway, breathless with excitement. "I never dreamed in a million years I would ever see something like this, let alone be able to live in it." She was running from room to room and looking at the magnificent view. "Look at this kitchen, and oh goodness, look at the size of the rooms. You are truly an amazing man, and I must say I am so proud of you and your achievements. My only heartache is my poor sister Hannah and her lovely children."

"I have told you, Zelda, please do not bring it up again. They will always have a home with us. Look around you. There are plenty of bedrooms. Now I have taken Sol into the business, and he has his own little family to take care of. I have taken Ada into the showroom, and she is now seeing a young man. They are all growing up, Zelda, so do not worry about any one of them."

"What are you talking about? We have our Sarah still unmarried, Esther just engaged, Becky, and now our baby David. Hannah's Harry, Ada, and Morris. I cannot understand my brother-in-law leaving them all these years, missing the best part of their lives. He writes, saying he nearly has paid for this house and he will soon want them to come. I do not think for one moment his children will want to go now. Their lives are being made here. I just don't know what will be."

"I have asked Harry to go to the South of France to work with Sol there. I think expanding the business will be very beneficial to our family."

"Leon, you have some kop [head] always for business that I never know what you are thinking of next. This is wonderful, darling, and yes, I love the apartment, love it. When do we move?" Laughing, she went over to Leon, ran her hands over him, and said, "Shall we make love now?" pulling her dress over her head and coming toward him with just her underwear on. He felt himself harden like a brick. Their lovemaking had always been very passionate, and he had never had to look elsewhere.

Now they fell to the floor, entwined in each other's arms, hastily removing the rest of their clothing. She climbed on top of him whilst he struggled to put his penis in her. "It is too damn awkward like this," he shouted as he moved her onto her back, and they both screamed with ecstasy, no foreplay. They were both too excited.

"I cannot believe that I let myself go like that. We did not have to worry about anyone hearing us. What a difference that makes. I am always so nervous of making a noise. There is always someone there."

Zelda was clinging to him, and so they lay in each other's arms until Leon said, "I really have to get going now, take you home, and then go on to the shop to see what is going on there. Wow, what an afternoon this has turned out to be. Make all the preparations to move. It is not necessary to rush. I know you have so much to do with the new baby, so let us say two weeks, which will be July 12th."

When she got back to the apartment, she went straight to her bedroom and checked on the baby as he lay fast asleep. She touched his face. "My beauty, I love you," she said in a whisper and then went to see what her sister Hannah was up to. She was lying on her bed, crying.

"Good grief, what has happened?" Zelda rushed over to her sister's side.

Hannah turned her back and sobbed. "I don't know what to do. After all these years, now the children have grown, he wants me to come." She held his letter in her hand and continued, "He has always written to say he wants only the best for us and will save every penny to buy his own property. I admire him for this, but to leave us all these years is also unforgivable. I still love him, yes, I do, but the children are adults now. I have to sit down with them and see how they feel about going. Oh, Zelda, he says he has bought a beautiful house in Lakewood, New Jersey, with a nice garden. It is his. He bought it right out. There is a large Jewish community, and the rabbi said he would be delighted for us to join their services."

Zelda felt her whole day of happiness fall before her. "When does he want you to come?" Hannah was part of her life. They had always been together, and the thought of her going away brought tears to her eyes. "I just cannot imagine my life without you."

"That is the biggest problem. He sent a money transfer by Western Union payable to me so that I can arrange the voyage for us all. Do I know if Ada, Harry, or Morris will go? I feel I could not go now Momma is not well. Aunt Anna has never been the same since Uncle Dov died. If I was to go off and perhaps never see them again, you know I go every day to cook a meal for them every day. Bless their hearts. No, I am not going to do it. We will have a family talk though. I will give the children the opportunity to go if they want to. I will not step in their way. I am going to stay with you, Zelda, as long as Leon does not mind."

"Absolutely he does not mind. We were only talking about you today because he took me to the most magnificent apartment. We are all going to move. You have a special room with a balcony overlooking the Seine, and there is room for everyone. He feels you and the children are part of his family, and he would not have it any other way."

Starting dinner for all the children and themselves was a big thing every day, but whilst Zelda was out,

Hannah had put on a nice chicken soup and had made some lokshen (vermicelli) to go in it, had already made a large salad, so they started peeling some potatoes and put them in the oven with a large piece of beef to roast. David by this time had woken up, so Zelda quietly went to feed him whilst Hannah finished the preparations.

By the time the family settled down to eat the beautiful meal they had prepared, Hannah felt calm herself, so after serving the soup to everyone, she said, "I have an announcement to make."

Everyone fell silent except Ada. "Oh, come on, Momma, are you pregnant?" Everyone laughed.

"Stop with that fresh mouth, Ada. First of all, you all know how things have been with my husband, your father, so far away and always we have thought of joining him in America. Now he has sent the money for us to go, and I will leave it to you, Ada, Harry, and Morris, if you want to go. My decision is I will not. My obligation now is to stay with Booba [Grandmother] and Aunt Anna as they are old and if I go, I may never see them again."

"What are you saying, Momma? That we should go without you?" Harry was looking astonished. "Uncle Leon has offered me a fantastic position working with Sol in the South of France. No, I do not want to give up my life here, family, and friends for what, for a father that I do not even remember. I for one am not going to do it." Scraping his chair, he stormed out of the room.

"I definitely do not want to go. I am working for Uncle Leon in the shop, and I love it. I am seeing Hymie, who wants to take me to meet his parents next weekend, and I am telling you all now if he asks me to marry him, I am going to. I love him, Momma. I hope you all understand my feelings."

Ada began to cry, and with that, Uncle Leon stepped in and said, "Ada, of course, we understand and, my darling girl, you are like my own daughter. We only want you to be happy. Hymie will make you a wonderful husband. He comes from a very good family here in Paris, and I know them very well. Let us wait and see first of all if he does propose to you."

Morris, sitting there very quietly, said, "Momma, I have been in and out of jobs since leaving school. I know I never met my father, but I would really like the opportunity of going and seeing if I could make something of my life. I seem to be floundering right now, so maybe this would give me the opportunity to make something of myself and to see the world. I have always grown up with the knowledge that one day I would go, so may I, Momma? Do you mind?"

"Of course, I mind, my precious one, but you are your own man now and a bird must leave the nest and fly, so we will make arrangements for you to go with our love. I will write to your father with our decision. He will be very disappointed that we are not all coming but happy that at least one of the family will join him. The offer will always be open to all of you, I am sure, anytime."

Chatter continued around the table. Sol was excited about going to Cannes, by which time Harry had rejoined them. The girls all got up to help clear the table. Esther said to Sarah in a low voice, "Can you believe he has actually asked them to come after all this time? I do not blame Aunt Hannah refusing to go. If I had a husband that did not care for me all those years, I would have divorced him."

"Do not be stupid, Esther. Jewish women do not get a divorce. It is a shanda [disgrace]," Sarah indignantly replied.

When Hannah visited her mother and aunt the next day, she made them something light to eat. Both had not been feeling well. In fact, when she got there, they were still in bed. "Come on, you two, get up. It is a lovely day, and I have brought you some nice goodies to eat."

When they were up and dressed, sitting at the table with some food, she told them of the arrival of the letter with money from Benjamin and of their decisions. "I did not influence the children in any way, but they as adults had to make their own choices. I had made up my mind that I would definitely not be going, so I made that perfectly clear.

"All these years, he has scrimped and saved for a beautiful house. Now he wants our children to give up all their friends and family for this stupid dream of his, and they do not want to do it. However, Morris wants to go, which will obviously break my heart, but he is old enough to choose to do his thing and I must let him go. Both Ada and Harry do not want to go and are very much involved with their lives here."

"Oh, our poor beautiful Hannah, sad that he went off for all those years, but at least you had three wonderful children from him. His misfortune in life not to have the pleasure of seeing them grow up—what sort of a man is he? A great disappointment to us all and truthfully, you are better off without him," Zena said very angrily, and Aunt Anna sat there nodding and saying, "You are better off without him. Thank God your children have grown into wonderful young adults, and yes, we will all respect their decisions."

A few years went by after Morris left for America. News of him was sparse, but Hannah was happy to learn that his father had introduced him to a friend who manufactured some kind of adornments which they called jewelry. He had now finished an apprenticeship and was quite excited to start work.

He was staying in the house in Lakewood on Friday and Saturday; however, during the week stayed in New York as he had a little one-bedroom there so it was easy for him to get to work. Rabbi Gunterman had been wonderful to him; he had introduced Morris to his daughter Rachel, and Morris fell instantly in love with her.

Preparations for the wedding took place, and Morris wrote to his mother about this wonderful event in his life. Now he was working a full-time job. They would marry next month, and he hoped his mum could make the trip over to be with them. She could stay at the rabbi's home. Benjamin, for his part, had told the rabbi that he was prepared to sign over the house to his son once they married, and please God the young couple should be very happy there.

After Anna passed away, Zena moved in with her daughters Zelda and Hannah. Aaron, the youngest child of Anna and Dov, had been working in the furniture business, when he was approached by the owner. "Are you willing to go to England? We are about to open a showroom there. We are needing someone like you to run it and be in charge."

After that, he had tossed and turned many a night, thinking, "Shall I ask her to marry me? It is such a great opportunity, one that may never come my way again. Do I love her? Yes, obviously I do, as I feel I do not want to leave her."

Decision made, he went round to Lena's parents and asked for her hand in marriage.

Excitement reigned in both families, and arrangements had to coincide with his job. "Where will you live?" Lena's father wanted to know.

"The company is opening this showroom in Whitechapel, which is in the East End of London, and we will be given the apartment above the showroom."

"A mensch [good person], thank God my daughter is blessed. May you have years of happiness together."

When he told his family of his intentions, Zena said, "He will go under the chuppah on my arm. My dear sister-in-law Anna and brother Dov, may they rest in peace, would be very proud that he found such a lovely girl and will be going to try his fortune with her by his side."

On the day of the wedding, all the women congregated at the bride's home. Lena looked exquisite. Very petite, she was dressed in an ivory-colored fitted dress high up to the neck, with long sleeves. Her bouquet was made out of large lilies, and she had her young nieces as her bridesmaids, all dressed in the same color as the bride.

Sitting on a comfortable seat, which was covered in a white sheet, she greeted the women as they came in. Each person was in awe as to how magnificent she looked, when Hannah's voice in the doorway started saying excitedly, "Come, come, it is time to go." She felt so much a part of this wedding, as unfortunately, she had missed it with her own son Morris in America. The synagogue, which had an adjacent hall, was just around the corner, so the bride on the arm of her father and mother, bridesmaids, aunts, and close friends following her, walked the short distance with all the neighbors out looking and shouting, "Mazel tov, Lena, be happy."

Zena had gone to the synagogue a little earlier so she could walk Aaron down the aisle. He would be waiting for Lena under the chuppah. All the men were seated already when a hush came over the congregation and the bride was taken to another room. Aaron left the chuppah to inspect Lena raising her veil as was the custom. Was this or was this not his intended wife? Smiling, he nodded and left the room and so the service began.

Both Lena and Aaron had been brought up in very religious homes. As they set out on their journey to England, Lena said, "My mother was so good with cooking and keeping milk from meat. I will have no one to show me right from wrong." And she burst into tears.

"Do not worry, my love. It is all the excitement of the wedding. We will work it out as we go along. I am sure there will be people to ask, and plenty that will be willing to help you. Straight away we will join a synagogue, and we will both make friends. Do you love me? That is the most important question of the day."

Looking up into Aaron's eyes, she replied, "I love you. Never doubt it. Otherwise, what am I doing here?"

They both laughed. The tension of the wedding and preparing for the journey eased as they saw their new apartment. "I never dreamed in a million years we would have such space: a kitchen, bedroom, and another room, which we can have as a sitting room. So nice, Aaron, and how convenient, right over your shop. I know we will be happy here."

The apartment was already furnished; the company had even had cooking utensils in the cupboards. They had nothing to think about but their bedding, which they had brought with them. People had been buying them wedding gifts, so they virtually did not need a thing, a wonderful way to start. Most couples would only dream of such a beginning.

Someone came and knocked on their door, a young woman who introduced herself. "I am Rachel Finkelstein. We were told you were coming today, so I have been waiting for you. I am the rabbi's wife from Fieldgate Street Synagogue, and I am here to help you in any way I can. The synagogue is just around the corner from here. We have a wonderful congregation and hope that when you are settled, you will do us the honor of joining us. In the meantime, I have brought you some rolls and challah bread, butter, eggs, and milk. I will not intrude upon your time, but please do not hesitate to call on us tomorrow so we can advise you on the area, where the baths are, and where to shop."

"Oh yes, I do appreciate it so much," Lena said. "Thank you, there is so much I need to know. We have only just got married, and now we have left our family in Paris I was feeling very down until you arrived."

"No problem, please come for breakfast in the morning. The rabbi, my three children, and I are at #90 Fieldgate Mansions temporarily until our apartment is ready at the back of the synagogue. Just turn onto New Road, and we are the first street on your right. See you tomorrow, then."

"Isn't that wonderful, Aaron? She seems so nice. So young though, with three children, and I really think she looked like she was pregnant with a fourth."

Aaron put his arms around her. "We will have our own family too one day, but enough talk. I cannot wait to get you into our own bed and make love to you, so let us make up the bed and really start our life together here in London."

Both laughing, they unpacked their bedding and flopped down on the bed, and literally fell asleep in each other's arms. Waking up in the middle of the night, Aaron got up to relieve himself, and smiling at the sight of his lovely new bride fast asleep, he curled up next to her and decided their lovemaking would have to wait until tomorrow.

When they awoke in the morning, they got a basin of water and washed and hurriedly dressed so they could go round to the rabbi for breakfast. "We will have to put our desires on hold, my beauty, until later, but do not fret. We will have our romp this afternoon. I am just lucky I have a few days off, so we can explore the area together and explore each other. I am just the luckiest man here in London."

"Oh my goodness, promises, promises. However, we were both so exhausted last night, anyway. We have our whole lives ahead of us and, I am sure, plenty of lovemaking."

Laughing, they walked together to meet the rabbi. Rachel was at the door to greet them. "Come, come, we have been waiting for you. This is my husband, Rabbi Joseph Finkelstein." Guiding Lena in, the men shook hands and started talking straight away. Lena felt very drawn to Rachel and so their friendship began.

Rachel introduced her little ones: David (aged four), Nathan (three), and Aaron (two). They were all dressed the same, with a little white shirt and navy trousers. They looked so adorable that Lena fell instantly in love with them. Everything was spotless, although Rachel said that it had been hard living there as their kitchen was out on the landing and their bedroom too, which at the moment the boys had to share with them until their apartment was ready at the back of the shul (synagogue).

"We must not complain though, as there is such poverty here that it breaks my heart. Only yesterday, one of our ladies was beaten by her husband. He had turned to drink as he could not get any work, and she was wanting money to feed the children. Joseph went to talk to him, and I made two chickens and some soup and sent it round to them. Sometimes it makes me feel so desperate. Thank God we have a wonderful group of ladies, whom you will meet, and they help tremendously."

"Once I get settled and meet people, Aaron and I will join and do whatever we can to help the community. That sounds so awful I cannot imagine living like that."

They were sitting around the table. They had orange juice, cereal, and bread and jam. The boys were sitting nicely. Rachel was spooning some cereal into Aaron, but otherwise, the others were all managing themselves.

"This is our usual breakfast. I find with the boys at this age, I do not do anything fancy, and this way, they know this is what they get and I do not have them shaking their head, they do not want. The only choice is the jam. We have strawberry or marmalade. Their favorite is the strawberry."

"Well, it is wonderful that you have given us the opportunity to join you, and I really want to thank you. You have such a lovely family, and I hope we can be good friends. I do not know anyone here at all, so you will be my very special friend."

Aaron was telling Joseph, as they were on a first-name basis, about his plans for the shop, and Rachel was explaining and giving directions to the baths and the mikvah, also how to get to Petticoat Lane to the market and where to shop.

"So much to take in—however, Lena, I am here just around the corner, so anytime you can just come round and we can talk and perhaps have a cup of tea together."

They bade their farewell, thanking them both once again, and Rachel bent forward and gave Lena a kiss on the cheek. "Remember I am here."

As they walked away, Lena had tears in her eyes. "They were so wonderful, and she is so kind to everyone. I will try to help when we get settled. What are we to do now, husband? What are your plans?"

"First we go back to our apartment, get our towels and fresh clothes, and we will go to the baths. After our journey yesterday, I feel grimy. I just want to soak myself in water, and even though we stayed our first night in a hotel, I never got enough of you, young lady.

So watch out, and all I can say is let us go forward and hurry up about it."

When they reached the apartment, he laughingly drew her in his arms, gave her a lingering kiss, and said, "This is just a promise. You are going to have to wait until later. Come on, let's go."

With not a care in the world, life was wonderful and they both felt blissfully happy, and that was how they started each day. Aaron went down to the shop, and Lena did her thing, tidying up and then walking round to Rachel to see if she needed anything as she was then going shopping down the Lane, as Petticoat Lane was shortened.

Rachel told her, "I am four months pregnant and hope this time I will have a little girl. I love my boys to madness, but I hope I can have at least one daughter."

"What do you mean 'at least'? How many children do you want?"

"Want, want, not for me to decide—it is whatever our dear God will allow me to have. After Aaron was born, there has been a two-year gap. I do not know why, but somehow, I did not fall pregnant. Now we will be blessed with another child. Boy or girl, of course we will love it, but I should bite my tongue to say I hope it is a girl. What is the most important thing is it should be healthy, and that is all I must pray for."

With a little order from Rachel, Lena set off to the Lane. She stopped at the bagel lady first. She bought nine. Rachel had wanted six, and she bought the extra three for them. Aaron could always eat two anyway.

Then she went farther into the Lane. On the corner of Toynbee Street was a lovely shop that sold pickles and herrings. There was a big barrel of pickles outside, and she had to buy an extra one so she could walk down the street eating it.

Heading back with some herrings and smoked salmon for both Rachel and her, she dropped off the purchases to her friend. Rachel made her a cup of tea, and Lena had played with the children for a half an hour when she said, "I really must make a move now. I want to make some lunch for Aaron. He is stuck in the shop and cannot leave in case a customer comes in. So far, thank God, he seems to be happy and it is going well. I miss my family terribly though, but bless you, my friend. Without you, I do not know what I would do. I love Aaron. He is a caring and wonderful husband. Oh, I think I must be in a mood today. Take no notice of me."

"Do not be silly. That is what friends are for. One has to vent one's feelings. Please God once you start your family, you will have so much to occupy your mind there will be no time to fret. Do you have a doctor yet? I will give you the name of ours, so you could register with him."

Taking the piece of paper from Rachel, she went home to make Aaron his lunch of smoked salmon and bagels. There was a letter slipped under the door for him from Hannah, so she took that down to him at the same time as his lunch. When she came into the shop, however, she saw he was busy with some customers, so she slipped into the back office and left the lunch on the table with the letter and went out of the shop, intending to go back later to see him.

Going back upstairs, she was busy preparing their evening meal when all of a sudden, Aaron came in, going straight over to her and taking her into his arms. He was crying and telling her, "Aunt Zena has died. She was like a mother to me. We all lived together, and she was always there for me. I thank God, Lena, she had the pleasure of walking me down the aisle, I loved her so much, and that she had the opportunity of meeting you, my lovely bride."

"Come sit down. I will make you a cup of tea and a piece of yeast cake I bought this morning. It is lovely and fresh."

"I feel so bad that I was not there for her funeral. I will light a Yahrzeit light for her and go round to Joseph for services this evening and say Kaddish [a special mourners' prayer]. I will close the shop early this evening. I really do not feel I can concentrate too much right now, so I will go back down for one more hour and then close. I will put a notice on the door that I will reopen 9:00 a.m. tomorrow."

"At least you do not have to answer to anyone. You are a good salesman. Otherwise, they would not have given you this responsibility of the showroom in the first place. Your sales figures are good, you say, better than they projected, and you have only been doing this such a short time. Go, my darling, and I will carry on with making a nice dinner for you."

The following day, Aaron woke up to hear Lena being very sick. "What is wrong? Perhaps you ate something yesterday and have an upset stomach." Tears were rushing down Lena's cheeks as she could not control the feeling of more vomit, but actually, nothing more was coming out of her.

Aaron, with his arms around her shoulders, guided her to a chair and went to get her a drink of water. "See how you feel in an hour, then if you do not feel any better, we will go see a doctor."

"Rachel gave me the name of their doctor, so perhaps we could go and register with him. I have not been feeling myself for the last couple of weeks. Maybe I am coming down with a tummy bug or something."

"I will prop up the pillows for you. Come back to bed but in a sitting-up position, and maybe you could try to doze off for a little while. At least you do not seem to be sick now."

Falling back to sleep, Lena lay peacefully, so Aaron got himself up and dressed for work, writing a little note for Lena so that she knew he was only downstairs. He left with a worried feeling, but realizing there was nothing more he could do for her, he decided he had to start his day.

Having no assistants in the shop to take over, it was all his responsibility to sell. Placing orders had come easily to Aaron, and to expedite delivery had become a hard project. Overcoming this was indeed a big project, but his figures had been good for the short time he had been there. Word had come through from his head office in France: "Well done," so he felt very good with his efforts.

Midday, Lena came breezing in the shop, came over, and gave Aaron a kiss. "I really apologize. I really do not know what happened to me. All I can think of is I must have had a tummy bug. I feel absolutely fine now though, so just to let you know, I am going round to Rachel and the children. She is so busy now organizing their move soon. I try to help as much as possible. She is some remarkable woman."

"What about you, my love? You are the most remarkable of all." Aaron reached out, and giving Lena a hug and a lingering kiss, he patted her on her behind. "I am so happy to see you feeling so much better, and with some color in your face. You was so pale and drawn this morning you made me really worried. Say hello for me. See you later, darling, but if you do not feel good, come home straight away."

Making her friend a cup of tea when she arrived, Rachel had been busy packing and organizing her things. "I am pleased to have time out, so sit. Are you all right? You look a little pinched." Lena burst into tears. "I was so ill in the night, violently sick, so I must have had a tummy bug. Aaron was so wonderful and kind. Thank you, Rachel, for being here and listening to me. This is when I really miss my family."

Rachel, listening to her, went over and put her arms around her and hugged her and said, "I am always here for you. Now tell me, what have you eaten today?"

"Nothing, I thought I would give my stomach a rest. The thought of anything just makes me feel nauseous."

Aghast, Rachel went to the cupboard and gave Lena a couple of biscuits. "Eat these with your tea whilst I get the children ready. We will take the pram and go for a walk to Settles Street. I will show you how to get there, and if my doctor is open, you can go in and register and make an appointment."

They stopped in to Aaron first on the way to the doctor. Aaron thanked Rachel for going with Lena, but Lena assured him, "I am now feeling better. This was just for peace of mind that if we are ill, we have a doctor we can rely on. Diagnosing myself, I must have eaten something that disagreed with me, so I will come in to you on our way back." Giving Aaron a kiss, off they went with two of the children in the pram and David holding on to Lena's hand. There were plenty of people out and about, so no way was she loosening him. Although he did not like the idea and wanted to run ahead, they were able to bribe him with a lollipop.

Dr. Martin Feldman was an extremely to-the-point but kind man. He took down all her particulars, asking her such embarrassing questions about her periods and sex life that she started blushing. "Do not be embarrassed, my dear. If I am to be your doctor, I need to know absolutely everything about you, and I mean everything."

"I have been married now for two months. We came here from France, and I came with my husband, leaving all my family there. I have been feeling queer for the last few days, nothing I could say, other than a little sick. But this morning, whatever was troubling me, I brought it up. Perhaps I caught a bug. Anyway, Doctor, thank you for seeing me. Rachel thought I should register with you."

"Well, my diagnosis of you, young lady, is you are pregnant. From your last period date, I am estimating at least six weeks. I do not want to examine you at the moment as it is early days and I do not want to bring on a miscarriage. Take it easy, do not lift unnecessarily, and if you continue with this nausea, come see me again. Otherwise, come with your husband in four weeks. Nice meeting you, Lena, and I wish you mazel tov."

Rachel was waiting with the children in the waiting room when she came out. "Well, what did he say? Are you all right? You have gone deathly white. Here, come and sit down."

"No, no, I am fine, just a little in shock. He believes I am pregnant. I did not think I would get pregnant so quickly. We have been trying to be careful as we thought we would give ourselves a chance to get settled and used to each other first."

"Come, little one, let us start to go home so you can tell your husband your wonderful news. Mazel tov to you both, and I am going to say there is no being careful. Welcome your husband into your arms, and you will enjoy your family. If you will always worry about getting pregnant and push him away, you will not have a happy home. Love and make love and enjoy it. I will always be there to help you, so now consider me as part of your family."

"Thank you so much, Rachel, it is just the shock of it and obviously I am excited and yes, thrilled. We were talking of one day starting a family, and here it is. Yes, it is all happening."

Someone came running up behind them, pushed Lena, and snatched her bag. Screaming as she fell, she clutched her stomach to protect herself, and thankfully, she just scraped her knees. "We will have to send for the police—what a day. Are you all right though?" Someone came out from one of the houses, with a chair and some water, and Lena, now crying, thanked them so much.

The policeman, a burly man with a thick Cockney accent, went over every detail with her. She had not seen him. He had come running up behind her, and all Rachel could describe was his back. He looked like he could have been in his twenties, medium height, and he had a cap on, so she really could not say about his hair.

"Now think carefully, miss, what you had in your bag. Any papers to say your address, any ID whatsoever, did you have keys in your bag?"

"Yes, I had a letter from my mother in it and of course the envelope with my address."

"Well, first thing is you must have your locks changed immediately, I know of a locksmith. Here is his name, so get your husband to see him as soon as possible. Otherwise, it is not safe for you to be there. We cannot appoint a policeman to stay with you

24/7, but we have had a spate of robberies like this and then home invasions, so my advice to you now is to hurry along and we will be in touch, young lady. Hopefully, we will catch him and perhaps retrieve your belongings."

Hurriedly, they walked away. Lena was so anxious to get back to Aaron to let him know of all the happenings of the day. "Do you think this locksmith will be able to do this today?"

"Do not worry, Lena. I am sure Aaron will have it in hand immediately. You have a good man there who only wants the best for you. God bless the both of you, and your new baby in good health."

Rachel gave Lena a kiss and said she had to hurry home to see to the children's food. They had been out longer than she had anticipated and were getting irritable and also needed to be changed. "You go in and tell Aaron everything, good luck with the locksmith. I will see you tomorrow, bye for now."

Lena entered the shop, which had thankfully no one in at that time. She went straight over to Aaron and put her arms around him. Looking into his eyes, she said, "Mazel tov, you are going to be a daddy." The look on his face was astounding; however, she straight away told him of what happened after she came out of the doctor's and that he must straight away get a locksmith.

"Right, you stay here, darling wife. I will go round and see him immediately. We will take this in hand, so do not worry. If anyone comes in the shop, just tell them to take their time and look around. Your husband will be back in fifteen minutes."

Aaron came back with the locksmith, and Lena went upstairs to the apartment with him so that he could do the work. Thankfully, when he left, she went to make herself a cup of tea and just had to lie down, after which she just drifted off to sleep.

Lena wrote to her parents in France and said that this news had come a little earlier than they had expected. They were so excited to know that they were to become parents. She did not tell her mother, however, of her nasty experience, only that her friend Rachel, who was the rabbi's wife, had recommended her doctor, so she was being looked after. She would also have a midwife and, if needed, the London Hospital was very close by on the same road. This being the first grandchild for Lena's parents, her mother wrote back to say she would be coming over to England so she could help in any way she could.

Aaron straight away said he would put a bed in their living room to accommodate his mother-in-law, but once the baby was born, he would look for somewhere else to live so Lena would not have the stairs to worry about with a pram, and a little garden but most importantly in a safer environment. In the meantime, he would talk around, asking questions about different areas.

"My darling Lena, nothing in the world is more important than your well-being and of course our little wonder that is part of you and me, our family. I am so excited, and these months will go slowly as whether the baby be a girl or boy, PG he or she will be welcomed into this world with all the love we feel for each other. I am going downstairs to try to do some business now. What are your plans for the day?"

"I'm going round to Rachel now to see if I can give her a hand with the boys. She said Mrs. Brownstein was coming round this morning. She is the midwife, so I want to meet her as she is the one that will be delivering our baby PG."

Things were not going well in France. A lot of anti-Semitism was building up. The shop they had opened in the South of France had been doing really well, when one night, it was broken into and the thieves took everything, all the very expensive garments, wrote on the walls "Jude." This was enough for Leon. Money now was not a problem. He gathered his family around him and said, "Through the years, we have had to run from this, and now I am going to put my factory and shop in Paris up for sale. I will speak to my cutter, who is such an important part of my business, and I will take Sol, who has been the brains behind the shop. We will look into position and start anew." The look on everyone's face was amazement!

Leon said to them all, "Don't worry. Once we find something suitable in England as far as a factory is concerned, we will look for homes. I promise you all will have something beautiful. I have never been one to sit back and let things happen around me. I have made money and will not sit back and accept things as they are. Go home, everyone, think of what Papa has said. I love you all and will not have anything harm you."

Everyone was talking at once and coming over to him, with their arms around him and kissing him when he said, "Ginigh, ginigh [enough], there is so much happening in Europe that I do not like. I don't want any arguments. I just want you to do as I say."

Zelda left the room and went to their bedroom crying, saying, "This for what? How do we know what we will have? And my sister—I cannot leave her."

"Come on, Zelda. You know she and her family will always have a home with us. I have always said her family is our family. You worry, sweetness, my beautiful bride. Come give your husband a cuddle. Let me do the worrying for the family. In the meantime, you need to hold me tight. I have felt neglected as of late. It is about a week since we have had sex . . . Get those clothes off, and I will make you feel wonderful. I will lock the door!"

The following day, Leon, Sol, and Pierre the cutter started out for England, and the first stop when they got there would be to see his nephew Aaron. Hopefully, he would put me in the right direction of agents who would be in charge of factories. To his amazement when he did arrive they embraced, but Aaron had customers in the shop and Leon could not believe how busy he was. "Don't worry. We will take a walk and get a bite to eat . . . We have only just arrived and are hungry, so you carry on and we will talk soon."

They walked to Aldgate and saw across the street a big café. "Good," Leon said. "We will get something now." The menu was extensive. Sol and Pierre both ordered salt-beef sandwiches on brown bread, and Leon ordered chopped liver followed by borscht (beetroot soup) with potatoes in it.

Leon got up before the food started coming and went over to the people sitting by the counter. "Hello, my name is Leon. I wonder if you can help us. We are looking for factory agents and a decent place to rest our heads tonight as we are here from France and not familiar with the area."

Shlomo, one of the gentlemen sitting down, said, "Mr. Grodzinsky across the street is an agent. He has a sign outside. When you have had something to eat, go along and speak to him, and at the same time, he may recommend somewhere you may stay."

"Thank you so much," Leon said, "I am sorry to have interrupted your meal."

When he got back to the table, he explained everything to Sol and Pierre, and within a few minutes, their food was before everyone and they were absolutely famished so the boys ordered another sandwich each and a portion of latkes. Leon had finished his chopped liver, which came with brown bread, and now his borscht was before him with two big boiled potatoes, and he asked the waiter for sour cream. His booba (grandmother) always made it that way, so that was how he was used to it.

Once they had eaten, they went across to Mr. Grodzinsky and introduced themselves. They wanted to rent a factory manufacturing clothes as they had done in France, and they were told he had two available, one here on Whitechapel Road or one in Brady Street and that he would take them to see both. Once they had looked at both, they all agreed that the one in Brady Street would be too small but the one that was not far from Aaron in Whitechapel Road would be perfect. They saw there were enough space for the cutting area, machinists, pressing area, and finishers.

"I will take it," Leon said. "We will go back to your office now and sign the lease. Tell me when you want us to take over as we have to also find living accommodation for our families as we will all be coming from Paris. I personally do not want it until the first of the month. I have a nephew that has a business nearby if you need a reference. If you have an idea where we can put our heads down for the night, I would appreciate it."

"Right, let us go, and the first of the month will suit my company, and then you can go round to Mrs. Lubin. She lives on Fieldgate Street. I will give you the address, and you can talk to her, as she rents out rooms."

After signing the lease, Leon said, "We will just see my nephew briefly and let him know what we are doing.

Tomorrow, we will go to view houses so we will have somewhere to live. Perhaps when that is settled, we can buy the basic furniture from him and then let the girls decide what they want when we bring them over."

Aaron was so excited when they came into the shop. "Come, I'll close up and take you up to see my Lena. Her mother has just arrived from Paris as Lena is pregnant, and she will be a big help to her."

Aaron told his uncle that when the baby was born, he was going to look for a house or flat that had a garden. He was a very determined young man and said, "The business is doing very well. The company in France are very pleased with the amount I turn in each month, so they have given me a good raise. Where do you think you will look for a home? There will be so many of you that it will be nice to somehow live in the same area."

"We are going tomorrow. The man we leased the factory from said a lot of Jewish people have moved to Stamford Hill, Clapton, and Tottenham, so we will view a few in the morning."

Lena and her mother Mrs. Bloomberg were making dinner and invited them to stay. "Oh, I do not want to be an inconvenience," Leon said.

"It is our pleasure, and we are so excited to be able to have family here."

After meeting with the estate agent the following morning, Leon, Sol, and Pierre all gave their opinions and decided that if they bought a very big house on Filey Avenue, the girls could have a look around to see exactly what they liked themselves. This was a big sprawling house that could accommodate them all temporarily. "We will get three double beds in, plus a single for your little girl, Pierre, also for my sister-in-law. And as we get settled, the others, bless them, can come on afterward . . . Don't worry. We will each have a house."

Filey Avenue led onto Clapton Common, which was really beautiful, with a pond and seating around it, also a short walk you could be in Stamford Hill, where there was an abundance of shops: fish, meat, and grocery all mainly kosher as there were a lot of Hasidic Jewish people in the area. Leon haggled with the agent about the price and then, with a smile on his face, shook hands. "That is it. We take immediate possession. Let us go back to Aaron and see what we can get as far as furniture is concerned from him."

When they reached Aaron's shop, they told him what exactly they needed as far as furniture was concerned, plus a dining room. What could he recommend? "I will leave it in your hands. We will sell up everything in Paris and start afresh here in London as things are no longer good there. We will bring our patterns, and we will make whatever we can to make a pound."

That was enough for the day. They went on to Aldgate to that lovely café and indulged in a delicious meal.

Next day, they went back to the agent they leased the factory from, asking about machines that they might buy or lease.

"Here in England, you may pay extra on your rent, which is called paying off. Eventually, these items become yours, and you will need sewing machines, overlocking machines, hemmers, pressing, a table for cutting, and a cutting machine."

"That will help us out tremendously. I will advertise for workers once we come over and one step at a time," Leon told him.

To his son and Pierre, he said, "I think we have done enough here for now. We will go back to the girls and start selling up and arranging to ship out what is necessary, before which we will go back to Aaron and give him a key so he can get the furniture in that we need. We must have that part taken care of for our comfort."

On reaching Paris and telling everyone of all that they had achieved in such a short time, they put their flat up for sale, their factory and their shop. Money was not so easy to come by, and Leon had to take a bigger loss than expected. People knew that he wanted to sell and so were taking advantage and bartering with him on every detail! Irrespective, determined, one had to admit he was a self-made man, and no one or anyone would be able to change his mind.

Finally, the day came when they were departing. Hannah and Zelda hugged each other and were crying on each other's shoulders. "How can we leave such a beautiful flat?"

"Come on, girls. You will have a beautiful life and a beautiful home. I love you both, and you are very precious to me. Give me your support and encouragement. As you know, I will never let you down. When we get to England, you will be able to look around for a different house. If you do not like this one, I have made plenty of money in the last years, so we will have nothing but the best."

They took as many things from the factory as they could: patterns, materials, and even a dummy that they would be able to build their samples on all the time and which they needed desperately in the dressmaking factory.

Leon took a tremendous loss on everything. His expectations of what he could get were not reality in these times, 1914. People were talking of war, so they managed to leave in February and the war erupted in Europe in August. There had been winds of war for months. In June, Archduke Franz Ferdinand was shot to death together with his wife. The whole of Europe was in turmoil. Germany insisted that Russia immediately halt mobilization; however, they refused, so Germany declared war on Russia.

France urged Great Britain to declare support. Once Britain was involved, Leon went to the War Office, stating he had a factory and was capable of making uniforms and coats for the soldiers.

Time was flying by like a blink of an eye. Lena gave birth to a baby boy, Joseph. She was so happy to have family around her when she had the bris (circumcision), and Aaron was over the moon. Now was the time to start looking for a house for his little family. He immediately got in touch with the agent who had helped his uncle; however, it was not as easy as he thought. Property prices in general had risen because of the war, so when he went round to look, the agent suggested looking down the Hill, which was Tottenham, and took him to see three houses: Wargrave Avenue, Rostrevor Avenue, and Cadoxton Avenue. He made up his mind immediately it would be the latter. Just around the corner, on Fairview Road were two shops that had grocery to vegetables. You name it, they had it. Also on the street was an off-license selling any type of liquor.

It was a lovely day, for a change. They had a lot of rain for the last week, so Lena decided to have a walk, with baby Joseph all wrapped up and nice and cozy in his pram, round to see her friend Rachel. She was so happy to see her. Gorgeous Rifka was in her arms as she opened the door to Lena. "Oh, she is so pretty.

You must be so happy, Rachel, a little girl and in your new flat at long last!"

Rachel made some tea, then Lena started crying. "What is the matter? Tell me. I am distraught to see you unhappy, although after childbirth, it is quite a common thing to feel down. But look at Joseph. He is conanahorra [thank God] so handsome like his mummy and daddy."

"You are my best friend, Rachel, and I am going to lose you."

"You will never lose me. Come on, have your tea and let us talk about what is bothering you."

"Aaron does not want us to live in the flat above the shop anymore, now we have Joseph. He wants a garden so he can be put out there in his pram and get fresh air. He has gone with the agent to look at properties around the area where Uncle Leon is."

"Wonderful, you will make new friends, but we will always be friends. Do not cry. We will be able to visit one another . . . Look forward to new happenings. You have a husband that adores you and only wants the best for you and the baby. Yes, I will miss you living just around the corner from me, but I will also be looking forward to coming to visit you, and vice versa."

When Lena got home, Aaron was still not back, so Lena fed Joseph, who was being fed by breast, and was proceeding to burp him when Aaron burst through the door, so very excited!

"Darling Lena, I have found such a fantastic home for us to live in, and I know you will absolutely love it.

Your mother and father will be able to live with us and leave Paris permanently as they wanted to . . . We have two very nice bedrooms and one smaller one for Joseph. We have to help our families get out of France. With this war, who knows what will happen? My company has already asked me to look for furniture manufacturers in England as they do not know how long they will be able to fill orders. My cousins Yossef and Myer, cousins David and Harry have already been drafted into the French Army. I have not heard about your brothers, but believe me, they will not escape. Thank God Morris is in America and away from all this.

"Look at my wonderful son. Let me hold him for a while. I have missed you both today, but dear one, you will be pleased with me. It is a lovely neighborhood with a school and synagogue nearby. I know you will miss your dear friend Rachel, but we can visit. I am buying a car, so sometimes on a Sunday, we will do that. Next Sunday, I will take you to the house, then you can get an idea of what furniture we need. I'm so excited—our very first home."

Morris and Rachel Fishbein were very happy. Rachel's parents made the most magnificent wedding, for which they received so many gifts because of the fact Rachel's father was the rabbi and was so very well known. Benjamin kept his word and signed over the house on the lake to his son and daughter-in-law.

Perhaps in his mind, he was trying to make up for all the lost years.

Morris had worked hard going through his apprenticeship as a jeweler. They gave him odd pieces of metal to solder together then to bend it onto a sizing stick and size it to whatever size they told him. After a month of this, they had him learning to set stones. His fingers were nimble, and he soon found the knack of doing it; however, his English was not so good, making life rather difficult as they had to repeat themselves a few times.

By the time he and Rachel married, he could say he was now a professional jeweler. His apprenticeship actually had taken six months. Unfortunately, his mother Hannah chose not to come to the wedding. Talking to Rachel at the time, he said, "I love Momma so much, but how can we blame her? My father is in his own world, living with another woman, but he has really tried his best to help me since I have been here."

Morris travelled into New York to work, returning home on Friday before Shabbas (Sabbath), with Rachel preparing a lovely Friday night dinner, lighting the candles as was the tradition. Usually they went to the synagogue for Friday night services, but on this particular Friday, Rachel said, "Please, Morris, let us stay home tonight quietly by ourselves. We always have so many people around us, and we only have the weekends together." They snuggled up on the couch, and when Rachel was in the crook of his arm, she looked up at him and smiled. "We are going to be parents."

Morris jumped up with excitement. "Our own little family, I cannot believe it. Now you must not lift anything or try to do things when I am away. Find out if you can get someone to come in and help around the house. I am making enough not to worry.

"Who did you go to see, what did they say about sex? I do not want to do anything that might hurt you or the baby."

"Do not worry, my love. This is early days, so you cannot hurt the baby. I do not know how much into the pregnancy we can go, so I will find out. In the meantime, I have been to the mikvah (holy bath one would go to cleanse oneself), so let us take advantage of it and go to bed and make love to me. I have missed you so much this week. I never thought I could ever feel this way, but I do."

"I do not need an extra invitation. I cannot wait myself, just talking about it is making me hard. We will not do it through the sheet tonight. I just want to feel your body pressed up against mine. In the meantime, Monsieur is throbbing." Morris picked Rachel up in his arms and carried her into the bedroom. When they finally got their clothes off, he had to say, "I am so sorry, darling. Monsieur could not wait. I did not mean to climax so quickly. I promise in the morning we will make up for it and play a little."

"Come on, little one, let us get washed and dressed and go down to your father and mother and tell them our good news." They had just woken up, and Rachel was yawning and stretching, feeling very contented.

Morris, however, was up and already started his ablutions. "Come on, come on. I feel I want to shout this from the top of a high hill. I am so sad that my mother never lived to meet you. Yes, I am bitter against my father living with that other woman all these years . . . What did he want, my mother to come here and live in New Jersey and he would live with this Alice in New York? I cannot fathom his mentality!"

When they reached Rachel's parents' home, which was on Ninth Street, a nice walk from theirs, her mother came to the door and said, "Here is my little Rachella," which Rachel had always been called since she could remember. In fact, she told Morris her grandparents used to call her that.

"Momma, where is Poppa?"

"I believe he is in the study. I will go get him."

When he came out and saw them, his whole face lit up with a smile. "We were going to walk over to you two this afternoon. We wondered why we did not see you last night for services. Come, let us all have some lunch."

"Poppa, Momma, you are going to be grandparents." They all embraced, and Rachel's father the rabbi started singing, "Aye, Aye, Aye Mazel tov," with tears streaming down his face. He slapped Morris on the back and said how happy they were.

When Leon got home from work, there was a letter waiting for him from Harry. He wrote that thank God, they were all right, but he had to register for the army. All males over the age of eighteen were required. When being examined by the doctor, they had rejected him because of his club foot as he would not be able to march and fight. Harry had been with him in Cannes and was a terrific salesman. He now wanted to come to London as things were so bad in Paris. Could he find him a job?

> Dear Harry,
>
> Things are very different here. We have leased a factory, and because of the war, we have a government contract to make uniforms and coats for the soldiers . . . The only thing I could offer you at the moment is to be a presser. You will have to work hard, but you will earn good money and I will see that you and your family will have a nice place to live.
> Love to you all, write and let me know your decision.
>
> Uncle Leon

They all were really happy with the thought that Harry and family would come to England. The thought of any of their loved ones being involved in this stupid war was heartbreaking. Zelda said to Leon, "I hope we can get them all out. Where will they live temporarily until they get settled?"

Leon, in deep thought, did not answer immediately. "I think the best idea will be to speak to Aaron as since he and Lena have moved out of their apartment, maybe that would be fantastic if Harry could have that . . . All the furniture is there, so all they would have to do is move in all their possessions."

Next day on the way to work, he stopped off at the furniture shop and hoped to speak to Aaron; however, to his surprise, the shop was not open yet, so going on to the factory, he became very involved with what he was doing. When he stopped for lunch, he went down Whitechapel Road to see Aaron once more. They were happy to see each other, and when Leon explained what he had in mind, Aaron was delighted at the fact that Uncle Leon was offering him a job in the factory, after which Harry could always move on if he wanted to.

Leon wrote to Harry again, explaining all he had arranged, and that he should speak to his wife Bertha as this was a tremendous upheaval for his little family. But his two daughters were still very young; they would be able to adjust easily. Ada married last year and was pregnant. Leon wanted her to travel with Harry because her husband had been called up and was probably on the front lines. He wrote to say he would not allow her to be there by herself, so Ada agreed and would live with her mother until such time when they could be together.

Everything was arranged. They could not sell their things as no one wanted to buy anything whilst there was such turmoil around them, now that they were even enlisting married men to fight the Germans, who had a tremendous army. Taking a case each, they boarded the ship, all feeling extremely unhappy, not knowing what they would encounter at the other end, except that they would be reunited with their family. The journey seemed never-ending as Ada was very sick.

Finally they arrived in England. Leon met them at the docks, hugging and kissing them and saying how happy he was to see them safe and sound. The latest news was that the Germans had started sinking ships. There was no telling what they would do next. He told them how sorry he was for the rest of the family in France, but there was nothing more he could do at this time and probably things would get better and then he would try to bring them over.

He took them first to Whitechapel Road. The cupboards were filled with food. The family had bought a bed in the main bedroom, which the girls would have to share for the time being, which they called top and tail: a pillow at the top of the bed and one at the foot. As they were so little, they would be able to manage.

Leon said, "I have been in touch with Rabbi Joseph Finkelstein and his wife Rachel, and they assured me that they will be round tomorrow so they can welcome you and show you around. Harry, tomorrow rest. I know how tiring the journey was, but be ready on Wednesday. I will be here at 7:30 a.m. to take you to the factory. Bertha, on Friday, we will all go over to my house for Shabbas [Sabbath] dinner. The family are so looking forward to welcoming you both and your beautiful girls."

David had moved from Paris to Lyon with his girlfriend and had been living there for a few years. He was the youngest child of Leon and Zelda. When his parents moved to England, he had no intention of going. He was very much in love with Madeleine, and both decided against marriage at the moment because of opposition of both families because of religious grounds. Madeleine was just eighteen and David was now twenty-four, and they would hopefully marry when she did not need her parents' consent at twenty-one. Madeleine's parents were very much against the idea that their daughter would be living with a man. They were Catholic and David was Jewish. How could this be, what would the children grow up to be?

Love prevailed. They decided to move away from both parents. David was a carpenter, and it was not hard to find work. Sex was another thing. Their love was very passionate, but they both decided that they would be careful and he withdrew as soon as he felt he was reaching any climax. So far so good, Madeleine had not fallen pregnant, but who knows what will be!

All males had to register for the army between the ages of eighteen and forty-one. If not, they would face prison sentences. Looking at the letter that had just arrived, David felt his heart turn over. What would he do if they said he had to go? "I cannot leave you, Madeleine, here in Lyon. I have taken you away from your family, and you will be all alone."

"Cherie, if they say you will have to go, you must not worry about me. I will go back to my parents, whom I know love me and will not turn me out. My main concern will be for you to be safe! Once you register, they may not take you. Ask your company to write a letter that you are needed on the job. You never know."

David, the following morning, went to the registry office with the letter he had received. To his shock was the number of men there, all waiting to register. Once he reached the officer in charge, the officer said, "Join the line over there and wait to see the doctor to see if you are fit." David could not believe what his eyes were seeing and his ears were hearing. He tried to tell the officer that he was needed at work and he really did not want to join the army.

"Not interested, just go over there and stand in line. You are holding up all the people behind you."

With a lump in his throat, he knew he could not argue with this officer. Three hours later, he finally reached the doctor, who examined him briefly and said he was A1, fit to report the next day to be enlisted, get his uniform, and be prepared to move out.

That night, Madeleine clung to him, crying. He held her and caressed her, and as he hardened against her, she said, "Hold me, make love to me. I just feel I never want you to leave me." He rolled her over on her back, and as he entered her, he felt Madeleine's legs open wider and cross over his back pushing him in closer. He knew he was reaching his climax, but she would not let go. "No, no, do not stop. I need you now, and I do not want to think about anything else."

They clung together all night, and in the morning when it was David's time to leave, he said, "I have been so careful, but last night I could not hold myself back. Forgive me if I have made you pregnant. With or without your parents' permission, we will get married as soon as I get leave. I do not know what my pay will be in the army, but I will put you down as next of kin and send you everything I can. Just promise me you will go back to your parents. I cannot bear to think of you here without me and no family around. Any leave I have I will make my way to Paris. This way, we will be together whenever we can. Just remember, I love you with every fiber of my body." With a very passionate kiss, he was out the door.

Madeleine did not know what to do, decided to wait a few days in case when David appeared as instructed, they might tell him they did not need him. This crazy world we are living in, who knows what the next day may bring? However, if he did not come back, she was prepared to go back to Paris to her parents, irrespective of what reception she would get.

David reported to the barracks as instructed, stood in line for such a long time that his legs ached and he wanted to sit down; however, there were no chairs to sit on. Finally, he reached the sergeant in charge, who handed him his uniform and fitted him for boots. "What will I do with my own clothes?"

"Put them in this bag, seal it, and put your name on it. Go into that locker over there to change and then you will be shipped out for training."

After changing, he joined the other men already in uniforms and asked, "Do you have any idea where we are going?" No one had any information, so they waited. Trucks were coming and going all night, taking so many new recruits at a time. Finally around 3:00 a.m., it was his turn, and he was feeling like a sardine. The truck was jammed full.

On arrival, there was a sergeant major to greet them with shouting instructions, "You will be assigned to barrack G. Look for an empty bunk, and that will be yours whilst training. Go get some sleep as you will be awakened by me at 7:00 a.m., which will start your first day. I can assure you by the time I am finished with you, every bone in your body will ache and you will wish you never set eyes on me."

The next day, they were taken to a shooting range and were shown how to load a rifle and to shoot at a target. No one seemed to be doing too well as for most it was the first time ever with a gun. Then they were taken to a field that had barbed wire across it in lines. They were told to lie flat down and propel their bodies by their elbows to the other side of the field. If they were not flat enough, the barbed wire would be sticking in them. The sergeant major was shouting at them the whole time, "If I do not get you into shape, the Germans will polish you off, so put your heart and soul into it. You will be defending France. They are coming through Belgium, and now we have English forces going to join us at the front."

Their day seemed to go on forever. Sgt. Major Moreau made them march for miles with their backpacks filled with whatever they might need in the war and their rifles, which they were told could never leave their side. They were taught how to throw grenades and to look after and clean their rifles.

Finally, they were told to report to their mess hall so at long last they could eat. David felt that the bottom of his stomach was aching. He had never felt so hungry, but the sergeant major said they would get used to eating whenever they could. The Germans were advancing, and he was determined to shape them into soldiers and defeat the Germans.

David was shipped out after three weeks. Ready or not, they were all issued a knife and taught how to put the enemy in a choke hold and cut their throats. "Remember this, it is either you do it if you are in close combat or they will kill you. I have shouted and screamed at you to get you into shape because you are all nice kids. I want you to be able to come back to your families and live a peaceful life when this is all over."

It was raining heavily as the truck was going along. His thoughts were drifting to Madeleine and the last night they had together. When he could, he would write her and say just how much he loved her and prayed her parents had taken her back, in his mind, only temporarily because as soon as he got leave, they would marry especially if she was with child. He was sure they would certainly not object.

They drove through the night and he must have dozed off to sleep, but when they finally came to a halt, he woke up with a start, hearing gunfire and a new sergeant was now in charge of his platoon. He was not a pleasant person, and David took an instant dislike to him, but after hearing what was going on with the defensive battle of Marne, the French in combat had already lost one hundred thousand men within six weeks.

Sgt. Bolmundo ushered this new platoon into the trenches. They had a makeshift kitchen with coffee and tinned ham and baked beans, which they found out was going to be their diet from now on, after which he gave them positions to relieve the men standing guard. David found that he was standing next to men in the English Army some of the time. It was cold and damp. He was thinking to himself he needed an extra pair of socks on.

The Germans were bringing in heavy ammunition. They were prepared for the Germans to make their attack at any time when he started to make conversation with the man standing beside him.

"I am just sick of this war. We French have lost so many men already. I do not understand what the Germans want. Do they want to take over all of Europe?"

"Well, I certainly don't, coming over here and freezing cold. What's your name, mate? Mine is Solomon Sharpe. I'm from the East End of London, and I can think of one hundred things to do other than being here too. I cannot wait to get away from this vershtunkana [smelly, horrible] place!"

So a friendship developed Solomon discovered that David was Jewish. When they were relieved of their duties, they went to have a hot coffee together and commiserate about their woes! Some men had a severe condition called trench foot; this was caused through damp, unsanitary, and cold conditions. They communicated in Yiddish as neither spoke the other's language, and Solomon told David he could call him Solly as that was what the family called him, and because David had told him his mother and father were now living in London, a close bond developed between them.

David looked for him whenever he was on duty, but he did not see him for about a week and wondered where he was moved to. When he finally did see him, he said his brigadier general had moved them out on maneuvers. "We found some bloody Germans with their guns hidden in the woods over there, and we had to flush them out. Quite a battle, I can tell you, but we got them and got a few prisoners, who now have to be interrogated."

"At least you have seen some action—just standing on guard day after day is driving me and the other men out of our minds. We feel we would just like to charge over this damn trench and once and for all get them, but our sergeant major said that is why we lost so many men and we just have to be patient!"

As they were talking, a grenade was thrown into the trench, and Solly rushed to get it to throw it out and it exploded as he attempted to do so—yes, saving all the soldiers around him but killing him, and David standing next to him was very badly injured.

Solly belonged to the Royal Fusiliers. English medics came at once, covering his remains and taking him away to be buried. They said he was an absolute hero, saving everyone. David was heartbroken. They had put him on a stretcher and were taking him to the field hospital that was set up out of the line of fire. He was quite delirious, so he really did not know the extent of his injuries.

Morphine was in short supply, but they decided to operate on him to try to save his life but could not save his legs and had to amputate them. He was slipping in and out of consciousness. Who was around him and what they were saying—it was like he was looking down at himself and this was not real! He did not know about the amputation. He was asleep and then awake moaning and they gave him something and then was asleep again. He felt he was floating. Actually he was in a truck, being taken to a hospital away from the front lines.

Brigadier General Smith took it upon himself to sit down and write to Solomon Sharpe's family a letter of condolence:

Dear Mr. and Mrs. Sharpe,

It is with regret that I write today of the loss of your son Solomon. He died in the most heroic way, saving many men their lives. A most valiant soldier, and for whom I will recommend the Victoria Cross.

We gave him a military funeral and he is buried in Albert, which is a cemetery nearby. We will see that there is a marker by his grave and a Jewish star will be erected.

Sincerely,
Brigadier General Smith

The nurse in charge of David was talking to him, telling him her name was Dierdre and she would be there looking after him; however, David kept calling her Madeleine and holding her hand but then slipping back into oblivion again. Dierdre was in and out of his room. He had quite a fever, and she kept wiping his brow and putting water on his lips as they were so very dry.

When finally he woke and Dierdre was there holding his hand, she told him her name once again and that she was his nurse assigned to look after him as he had been injured. "Where is Madeleine? I thought she was with me."

"No, David, you are in an army hospital, and if you want me to write to her, I certainly will, to let her know where you are. Do you know her address and your parents'?"

He gave her Madeleine's address. "My parents will not be able to see me easily as they now live in England, but I do want to see Madeleine as soon as she can come. Thank you so much, Dierdre, how long have I been here?"

"One month in and out of consciousness, you thought I was Madeleine and kept saying how much you loved her, so it will be my pleasure to write to her now." With that, she walked out of his room before he could ask her too many questions about his injuries.

A few days later, there were horrendous screams coming from his room in the middle of the night. Dierdre rushed in and said, "Shh, David, what is the matter? Are you in pain?"

"No, I just woke up and I am tossing and turning, Nurse. I cannot feel my legs. What has happened to me? Am I paralyzed?"

Giving him an injection to calm him down, she put her arms around him and said, "Try to sleep now. We have really ill soldiers here that must get their rest, and we will talk in the morning." He was cradled in her arms, and she softly patted his head. His eyes began to close, and he seemed to be deep in sleep before she finally let his head rest on the pillow.

Dierdre knew that the time had come when she had to actually sit down and talk to David and let him know exactly what had happened to him. The following morning when she went in to him, he actually was just waking up. She brought a bowl of warm water, a facecloth, soap, and a towel and started to bathe him, when he grabbed her arm and looked her straight in the eyes and said, "Tell me, I want to know everything about my wounds."

Dierdre, with tears in her eyes, told him the truth and explained without the amputations on his legs he would be dead today. The surgeons managed to leave the thigh on both legs, so next week, he would start therapy by building his upper torso up with the rings that were above him, and the following week, he would be encouraged to swim and she would be with him all the way.

"Did you write this to Madeleine? How can she come to see me now? I am only half a man!" He started sobbing that his life was finished, and Dierdre put her arms about him and let him cry it out on her shoulder.

"Thank God you are here to tell the story. When you are strong enough, you will be able to be in a wheelchair and go up and down the corridors, chasing all the nurses. Anyway, it was only a few days ago I wrote to Madeleine. All the mail is upside down right now because of the war."

"Thank you for being so kind to me, but I have been thinking even if and when the letter got there, the parents would not let her see it. They hated me because I was Jewish and they Catholic, so they definitely did not want me for their son-in-law." Dierdre made up her mind at that point that she would try to find out the telephone number, perhaps she would be able to speak to Madeleine and explain what had happened; however, when she did, she found the number had been disconnected, so of course now there was no trace of them.

Speaking to David, she told him the truth. "They have moved away, David. You were right. They want no part of you. However, I have to tell you that you are handsome and your brain is good. You have strong arms and you will be able to love again. Yes, cuddle and certainly be loved and wanted."

Tears running down his face, he shook his head in defiance. "Who would want me now? And I would not want to burden anyone with me."

Dierdre held him tight. "I love you, David, and together we will make you strong and be able to fight these demons that are telling you *no* and make everything feel a definite *yes*."

President Woodrow Wilson went to Congress to vote for the USA to enter World War I. RMS *Lusitania*, a British ocean liner en route from New York to Liverpool, England, was sunk by German U-boats. He waited until April 6, 1917, but when news came that so many British merchant vessels had been sunk, he rightfully decided that no ship was now safe in the Atlantic.

The draft started for men aged twenty-one to thirty-one. Married men were excluded at first, but after a few months, they too received a letter from the conscription office. This now brought Morris with the letter in hand to Rachel, with tears in his eyes. Their little son Benjamin (Benny, as they called him) was running with a tiny toy car in his hand, and Rachel, now pregnant with their second child, was sitting, resting in a chair when he came in.

"I will go to your doctor and ask for a letter stating you need me here. You are not well and have no one to look after our three-year-old. Maybe, you never know, I may get an exemption. To hell with them all, these stinking Germans, goodness knows how it has been over there for my family. God, I would hate to go away and leave you, my darling, precious wife, but if I have no way out of it, then I know you have your parents and family nearby."

Morris went to the doctor and explained the situation. "No problem, I will write the letter for you immediately." After that, Morris took it the following day to the conscription officer.

"We are getting these types of letters all the time. When is your wife due?"

"Six weeks' time, sir."

"You will report back here two months after the delivery date. I'm stamping it on your papers. *Do not* mess about, young man, as I can assure you if you are not here, the military police will be knocking on your door!"

It was like they were living on eggshells. Their nerves were shattered. By the time little Abigail arrived, they were all feeling like they had been put through the wringer as all they could think about was Morris having to serve in the forces and being shipped overseas. Rachel's parents assured him they would move in with her so she would not be on her own with the children, and please God when he returned, they would go back to their own home. Abigail was so very beautiful, and was given the initial A after Morris's mother. "I'm so delighted we could do this for my mother, God rest her soul."

Time went by so quickly, and before he looked round, he had to report to the military. He had put his business on hold, had finished any orders he had to complete, and thought, "One day when I return, I will have a trade to come back to." Rachel stood at the door, crying with the newborn Abbie, as they called her, in her arms. Her parents stood very solemn-faced, wishing him well and a safe return and assuring him not to worry. They would make sure his little family would be in the best of hands. Benny, not knowing exactly what was happening and seeing his mother crying, held on to Morris's legs and was shouting, "No, Daddy, don't go!"

On Morris's arrival at the conscription office, they took all his particulars, and he was told to take a seat. If he wanted coffee, there was a machine there, and he was told to help himself as he had to wait for a truck to take him to which base he was going to be assigned to. There were two other men waiting at the same time. They all acknowledged each other and introduced themselves.

Hours went by before finally a truck came by and they were told to hop in. No one knew where their destination was going to be, but at this point, they did not care. Just to get out of these four walls, Morris felt such a relief when they were finally on their way! After hours and hours of driving, with an occasional pit stop to relieve themselves, they arrived just outside of Raleigh North Carolina, where they had a base and training facilities.

They were greeted by Staff Sergeant Williams, originally from Texas, with a very heavy Southern drawl. "Come on, you guys. We've been waiting for you all to get here. Follow me." They got out of the truck, stretching and yawning, when Williams started shouting, "If I say follow me, I mean now, not next week. Get your fat arses moving *now*."

They were ushered into a room stacked with uniforms, pillows, blankets, and every imaginable item a soldier might need, then taken to a barracks and told to change, after which Staff Sergeant Williams would be back to take them to the mess hall in one hour.

Morris, as he looked around after exiting the truck, was absolutely in awe. He saw rows and rows of tanks and lots and lots of soldiers hurrying along in different directions. "I don't know if I will be able to do this, and this sergeant, whatever his name is, thinks his shit doesn't stink. I pray to God to bring me home safely and in one piece." He was talking to himself as he followed. Once he was piled high with his issued items and taken to the barracks, he had a shower and changed into his uniform. He felt a little better, but terribly nervous.

Prompt to the hour, Staff Sergeant Williams came for them. "Follow me, men, to the mess hall, where you will be treated to one of our gourmet dinners. Bring the plate and the cup, knife, and fork you have been issued. You will be responsible for washing them and looking after them at all times. They will travel with you into action, and if you lose them, you will not eat."

When he reached the mess hall, Morris felt his stomach churning, not realizing how hungry he had been feeling until he smelled food. Now he knew to survive, he would no longer be able to remain kosher, so he tried to put it out of his mind. The menu was far from gourmet. You held your plate out, and a soldier who had kitchen duty and was dressed in white slopped mashed potatoes, chicken in some sort of gravy, and peas on his plate, then he could have tea or coffee or water.

Morris started eating, as did the other men, Morris first saying a prayer to himself, "Dear God, please forgive me. When I finally go home, I will be kosher again." He felt sick but absolutely forced himself to eat.

One of the men, Chris, who had traveled down with Morris, said, "Hardly like home cooking," and the other man, Brian, said, "I don't know how we are supposed to survive this goddamn war on this garbage." With that, they all started laughing, and a friendship was formed.

The next day, their training started. They found out that they were with the 110th Tank Corps, whatever that meant. They were not sure. They were shown how to load rifles and clean them. Captain Black came to speak to them how they were expected to salute any officer and how that was to be done. Rules and regulations in the armed forces were strictly upheld. If they did not salute an officer, they would be given punishment, which could be so many different forms that they would not wish to experience.

Everyone gazed at him in awe, but as this was their very first day, no one asked any questions. Their Tank Corp they had been assigned to consisted of hundreds of men, so they found out, from all over the country: New York, Montana, Utah, just to mention a few, and he even found out they had some Canadians there too.

The following day, they were on tank duty, holding their guns at the ready and walking behind the tank, using it as a shield. Captain Black was hollering out to them, "Get more behind unless you want your frigging heads blown off." He certainly did not mince words, but then this was no game. This was serious stuff!

After one week of intense training, learning how to shoot and load a gun, throw hand grenades and hand-to-hand combat fighting, they were on their way, feeling terribly seasick.

When will I ever have time to write to Rachel? They have not given us a minute to ourselves.

Other men were heaving over the side of the battleship. It certainly was a rough crossing. Morris could hold no food down, so he definitely did not go down to the mess hall. His friends Chris and Brian were not in any better shape, all feeling very sorry for themselves.

The journey seemed to go on forever. When they finally reached Calais, they disembarked onto land and transferred by truck into Belgium, where fighting was going on fast and furious. The German divisions were beating the hell out of the French and British soldiers. Now the GIs had joined the war with their tanks, they hoped to beat the shit out of them and make them retreat!

Captain Black was with them, and the very next day, their tanks were rolling, with them walking behind. "Keep your goddamn heads down behind those tanks. Otherwise, they will get blown to bits." Each had their helmets on, guns in hand and grenades ready for action. All of a sudden, it seemed all hell broke loose as the tanks were firing. He was shouting, "All right, men, this is your time. Do not let any of them get away."

The first aircraft were used in a pivotal role; however, by the time Morris was enlisted, machine guns were fixed to these aircrafts to create fighter airplanes. Noise above them was tremendous as the machine guns were finding their marks, making the German troops come out of their ratholes, as Captain Black described them.

Coming face to face with a German soldier, Morris was shaking. It was either kill or be killed. He saw him about to point his gun in his direction, and he threw his grenade with all his might. Captain Black was right behind him. "Good lad, give me your name in full. The colonel will be coming round later, and I will be sure to mention you to him. You not only saved your life but those around you."

It seemed all was quiet right now, so they were ordered to bunker down for the night. Tomorrow was another day. Americans coming into the war helped push the Germans back. Russia on the other side did their part, and the French and British soldiers, although somewhat depleted, were fighting alongside the Americans.

Now the year was 1918. The Germans finally surrendered. All the soldiers were being shipped back to their respective countries. Morris, all the way back, kept thinking of Rachel and how lucky he was that he was finally going home. He had got separated from his friends Chris and Brian; however, he found out they had both been ambushed and both did not make it.

His unit was sent back to Raleigh, North Carolina, which was their original training camp. The first chance he had, he wrote Rachel and said he would be home as soon as he was discharged and could not wait to hold her in his arms once again, to pick up Benny and Abigail. "Oh, will they remember me, as I want to hold them and kiss them all over. Maybe Benny will, but Abigail will not know me at all. And you, my love, my kisses will smother you. I just want to crush you to me."

Two weeks after arriving back in the States, he was officially discharged and thankfully in a truck heading toward New Jersey, back to his wonderful little family, his wife and children, and also his in-laws, whom he was extremely fond of.

In France, David was taken to an army rehabilitation center. Dierdre asked for a transfer so she could be with him. Leon had been writing to his son on a regular basis, asking him to come to London once he was fitted with his wooden legs. He would see he would have work doing all the bookwork for the company so he would be independent, with his own money.

Dierdre came into his room, all smiles. "Good morning, David, we are going for a lovely swim in the pool and then I am going to wheel you into the gardens so you can get some fresh air into those lungs of yours. You have been stuck in these rooms too long, and you are looking very pale."

David burst out crying. He was very emotional, which was certainly understandable. "My father wants me to come to England once I am fitted and work for him as a bookkeeper. Dierdre, you have become my life. I know it is wrong for me to rely on you for so much. I really love you and thank you for all you do for me. My feelings go beyond you being my nurse, which is so wrong. I'm only half of a man!"

With her arms about him, they were both crying. "If you are half a man, you are the very best. I will never think of you in such a way, and I have loved you from the minute I started working with you, David. You are amazing. I find you the most fascinating person I have ever been with. If you are even contemplating moving to England to be with your family and if they will have me, I would be honored to go with you."

They were holding on to each other and both crying when David said, "Darling Dierdre, if you could have me in such a condition, I cannot get down on my knees as I do not have them anymore, but will you marry me?"

"Yes, yes, a million times yes! We will work hard on these wooden legs, then we will start a new life together in England."

Life after that was definitely grueling for both David and Dierdre. They were both determined to make this work, and every time David lay back on the bed, he turned his head into the pillow and shouted, "No, no, I can't." With that, Dierdre said, with her arms encircling him, "You can, my darling. Yes, you can for me!" and held him until finally he turned and returned her embrace with a passionate kiss.

David wrote to his father, telling him of their intentions. They would marry in France when he was finally released from the rehabilitation center and could stand by himself. It was hard, but with Dierdre's help, he was well on the way of getting there. Amazingly, without his wonderful nurse and now future wife, he had given up all hope of living. Both looked forward to being with the family and, most important of all, being able to start their new lives together.

Everyone was returning from the War, Leon had changed his factory to similar work he had been doing in Paris, ladies' fashions specializing in petite, regular, and extra-large sizing, catering for all. They were busy, and everyone seemed happy except Ada, who had not heard from her husband for at least six months before peace was declared.

Ada was so distraught that she decided to write to the Ministry of the Home Office in Paris, giving his name and army number and asking them if they had any knowledge of Hymie Schubert as no mail had been received from him since at least six months previous to the war ending.

Some time went by when finally she received the following letter:

> Dear Mrs. Schubert,
>
> It is regret that we have to inform you that on September 16, 1917, during the battle of Verdun, your husband was captured, and we believe is a prisoner of war at this time. When further information will be on hand, we will immediately write to you.

Ada could not read any more. She started screaming, picking up little Golda, and running down to her mutter (mother). Tears streaming down her face, she pushed Golda into her mutter's arms and banged on their couch. "What can I do, what can I do? They have ruined our lives."

"Stop it. Look, you have made Golda cry. Can you stop now? You are even frightening me. Wait until Tate [Father] comes home. He will get in touch with the authorities, and he will get to the bottom of this." Ada called Leon Tate as through the years he was the one she had grown up with.

Leon came home to a storm of tears. "What is going on? Slow down, darling, show me the letter, and we will get in touch with Hymie's parents. We will answer this letter immediately, asking them for their urgent attention in obtaining his release. Shaineh maidel [beautiful girl], don't worry. You know how much we love you, and if I have to go there myself to bring him home, I will. Now go wash. Relax and go and have a lie-down. We will look after our gorgeous Golda (God bless her)."

After Leon had his dinner, he set about answering this letter and writing to Hymie's parents, asking them if they had any knowledge of what had happened to him, and if they heard anything, would they please write immediately to him as Ada was beside herself and signed it

Hashem yevarech otha. [May God bless you.]

Leon

Really he had no idea what else to do. It was a waiting game now, and Ada, his beautiful Ada, was not handling this well. He prayed she would not have a nervous breakdown.

After Leon left for work the next day, Ada came down with Golda. She looked like she had been crying all night. "Mutter, I am trying to be strong for Golda's sake, sorry if I went off the rails yesterday. Please God they will release him soon and he will be able to come home. He will be able to see a beautiful daughter whom he has never set eyes on, and thankfully this nightmare will be over. I am so thankful that you and Tate insisted I came over to live with you all. I do not think I ever want to go back to France again, but we will see what Hymie will want to do."

A total of six weeks went by before they heard from the French War Department informing Ada that Hymie Schubert had been released that morning from the German prisoner of war exchange and had been sent to an army hospital for evaluation. The letter being short and brief left an awful lot to the imagination. "We must all think positive, most of all, good thoughts," Ada said, hugging Golda. "Tate [Father] will be home soon."

Ada decided to leave Golda with her mutter and travel to her in-laws. Maybe then they could find out what army hospital Hymie was in. All sorts of thoughts were in her mind constantly, but just the thought that she was going over there and might be able to see him shortly cheered her immensely. "Mutter, I will go because I know Golda is in the best hands, hopefully,

I will be back in two weeks. I just must go to see him and just know he is all right."

"My darling maidel [girl], I will devote every second of every minute to her, you know I will. Go to your man [husband]. He is the most important person right now, and I know you will not be happy unless you do this."

When Leon came home from work, Hannah his sister-in-law had made her special dish. She knew he loved stuffed cabbage served over rice. Little Golda had been put to bed, and to his surprise, he found Ada in a much happier mood. "Well, tell me have you heard from Hymie. You seem like you have a big weight lifted off your shoulders."

"I want to go to France to my in-laws and find out where they have taken Hymie. Mutter said she would look after Golda for me. I need to go, Tate. I must see how he is for myself."

"No, I will not allow you to travel by yourself. Are you mad? Absolutely not! I cannot go with you as we are in between seasons, with orders we have to fill. You cannot go unchaperoned. What about Mume [Aunt] Zelda? Maybe she would go with you."

"Would you, Mume Zelda? I have to do this. How do I know what state he is in? It is ochen vey [terrible]. My mind is going all over the place, imagining so many horrible things they may have done to him."

"Your Mume Zelda has always been there for you, so *yes*, don't worry anymore. Leon, book the tickets for us. Maybe we can find out where David is and we can visit him too."

The next morning, Ada wrote to her in-laws, saying how worried she had been about Hymie and her mume had kindly said she would travel as her chaperone to France, and if it was all right, could they stay with them until she found out where he was so they could go visit him? Not knowing what his health was after being a prisoner of war was a nightmare to her. My Tate said he would be booking the passage for us, so we will leave enough time for you to receive this letter and we will arrive a week from this Sunday, please God.

Finally, the day came when they were to depart. Ada hugged her mutter so tight Hannah said "Go, go already safe journey and hopefully he will be able to join us all here."

Greeting them at the door was Bertha and Aaron Schubert. They hugged and embraced and ushered them into their living room "God bless you both for coming. We only wish it would be under better circumstances. We have been in touch with the War Office and have found out Hymie is in a rehabilitation hospital twenty-five miles from Paris, in Amblainville. We tried to say his family wished to see him and they did not advise it at this time, but we are going irrespective of what they say, so tomorrow morning if you are up to it, we will order the driver for 8:00 a.m."

Ada started crying, and Bertha went over and put her arms around her, saying, "Let all your tears flow today, dear Ada, because when you see my son, you and all of us must be very upbeat letting him know just how much he has been missed and how much we love him, giving him the encouragement to get better as quickly as he can. God knows what condition he is in. We could not get any specifics out of the authorities, and goodness knows what those German bastards did to him whilst he was imprisoned."

Zelda had been silent all this time and said, "We also must locate my son David. He had been near Paris, but they transferred him to a different location not too far out called Creteil. He had both legs amputated, however, mentally now he is doing fine. Apparently, he has such a wonderful nurse, and they love each other so much that as soon as they are able, they plan to get married and come to England. Oh, this damn war has torn families apart. Thank God it is over and Hymie will be able to be with his gorgeous wife and beautiful daughter. Ada, you brought pictures. Let us all see this little beauty."

After looking at the pictures, Bertha ushered them to the table, which she had already set in anticipation of their arrival. She had made fried and boiled gefilte fish, potato salad, coleslaw, and a hot rice dish with peas in it, absolutely delicious, and as everyone was hungry, they greatly appreciated her efforts. Dessert followed, which consisted of her homemade apple pie and strudel. Zelda and Ada thanked them so much for their hospitality and, after a little while, decided they would have an early night as they were exhausted.

The following morning, all washed and dressed Ada stood by the window, waiting for eight thirty until the driver arrived. Hastily, they all put on their coats, hats, and scarves and rushed outside into the bitter wind and cold. She felt sick to her stomach with anxiety. This was the moment she was waiting for but dreaded.

Mostly the roads were fine, although a slow drive as it was icy after the snowfall the day before. The driver did not have much to say other than he had to take it very easy. They had booked him to take them to this army hospital and to wait for them however long they would be.

Not having an appointment, they were astonished to see the barricades up and guards standing in their sentry boxes on each side. They pulled up in their car and said they were here to see Hymie Schubert and were asked if they had an appointment. After their response "no, they had not," they were told that without that, no admission would be allowed.

Ada got out of the car and started shouting and screaming at the guards. "I want to see whoever is in charge. I am his wife, and I have traveled a long way. I demand to see him and to know of his progress." With that, the guard got on the telephone to his superior, telling Ada that someone would be along to talk to her.

Getting back in the car, she told her in-laws what was going on and that they had to wait for someone to come and speak to them. With that, they could see an officer approaching the gate. Ada, Mume Zelda, and her in-laws all got out of the car. As the officer came upon them, Ada spoke, stating they had come to see Hymie Schubert, she was his wife and these were his family. Shaking his head, he declared, "I am sorry,

Madame Schubert. He is recuperating after severe shock, Doctor's orders are for no visitors."

"Well, we demand to speak to the doctor. I am not leaving here until I do so. Get on the phone, do what you have to do. I have traveled from England to see my husband and left my baby in my mother's care, so if you think I have come here for a joyride, you better think twice about it!"

Turning around, the officer went into the sentry box, and they could see him on the telephone, speaking to someone. He had turned his back on them, but from the movement of his arms, they could see he was very perturbed. Coming toward them, he said, "Normally, without an appointment, the doctor would not see you, but making an exception for you. Please drive in and go to the far building on the left. His name is Dr. Phillipe LeRoy.

Greeting the family, Dr. LeRoy asked the family to be seated in his office. Ada said they wanted to see Hymie and that this had been such a terrible worry to all of them and they wanted to know what treatment he was having and obviously what progress and when, most important, he would be able to come home. All these questions came tumbling out so quickly, but she could not help it. All her anxieties had built up to a crescendo point!

"This is quite unprecedented. I never see families without an appointment, but as you have all traveled so far, I will try to help you with any questions you may have. First, let me tell you what problems we have with Private Schubert, not just one problem but immense problems.

After being released from the prisoner-of-war camp, he believes that we are Germans and are trying to poison him. We have had to sedate him and feed him intravenously. Now he is having shock treatment, Mrs. Schubert. Even if we allowed you and you went to see him now, he would not know you. We have had many cases like this, and it takes at least six months of recovery."

"Does this mean you do not want me to see my husband, and his mother and father should not even see him?"

"I know how hard this is for you, Mrs. Schubert, but soldiers have come back from this damn war in terrible conditions. Your husband had malnutrition and was so thin he could hardly stand."

Ada by this point was crying, so her father-in-law stepped in and said, "Doctor, I do understand, but is it not possible for us to try to talk with him? Maybe it could help my son! My daughter-in-law now lives in London, and this ordeal has been heartbreaking for her. Even if she could see him and talk to him about their beautiful daughter, perhaps even show him some pictures?"

"I am so sorry, Mr. Schubert. Perhaps you could make an appointment with me for a month's time, and we can review the situation. Right now, only the male nurses are allowed in his room as he can be quite violent, thinking he is still in German hands. That is the best I can do for you. If you will excuse me, I have to make my rounds. Make an appointment with my secretary as you go out. Your son will get better, I promise you. Mental health is patience, patience."

They left the hospital with very heavy hearts; however, Aaron tried to be much more optimistic. "At least he assured us he would get better. Have hope, Ada. We will keep up the visits and appointments from this end. Now you must look forward to going to see your son, Zelda, keep a happy face. Thank God he has been spared.

The next day, they just rested. They felt they could not proceed without resting. After such a traumatic day, neither Zelda nor Ada slept and they were talking on and off all night. They arranged for the driver to come and collect them. At last, they were on their way to Creteil to see David, and they wrote to him beforehand to say they were coming.

Ada was holding on to Zelda as they approached the steps of the hospital. She was shaking, and when they went in, it was Ada that gave David's name and the receptionist nurse directed them to David's room. As they approached, Zelda held back but Ada took her firmly by the arm and said, "Kumen in [come in], *smile*, and make him feel this does not matter. What *does* is that he is here. Thank God, maybe not whole but still a person with feelings and a brain, *not* like my Hymie nebech [unfortunately]. Will they be able to help him? Who knows what my life will be? I cannot think further than today and seeing lovely David."

DAVID'S REHABILITATION

As they opened the door and they saw David, both Zelda and Ada rushed over and put their arms around him. David started crying, which set them all to be very emotional. In the background was Dierdre, and David held out his arm for her so she could be introduced. "Mutter [Mother] and my lovely cousin Ada, this is my one and only beautiful Dierdre, without whom I could not exist."

"Not true, darling David, you have come a long way, yes, with my help but mainly with your determination. Exercising, pulling yourself up by your arms and making your body strong, swimming every day, you have pushed yourself with every fiber of your body."

"Mutter, I love Dierdre, and when my wooden legs arrive and I am comfortable learning how to walk on them, we are going to be married. Tate [Father] offered me a job as his bookkeeper, which I know I would be good at, and Dierdre said she would get a job as a nurse. We would get a home that would be suitable, with a ramp for a wheelchair when I don't have my sticks on, which is what I call them." Everyone laughed, and it sort of broke the tension.

Zelda went over to Dierdre and put her arms around her, giving her a kiss on each cheek, and said, "I cannot tell you how very grateful we all are to you and the fact that you have made my son so happy. I will welcome you into our family with open arms."

Ada then started telling David about what happened to Hymie. "His mind has been shattered with what those bastard Germans must have done to him in the prisoner-of-war camp that now he believes everyone is German and that they are trying to poison him. His parents have an appointment with the doctor next month, and they will let me know of his progress. I will come back to visit him if I can when they say, but at the moment, *no* visitors are allowed and I cannot impose on my mutter to look after little Golda."

David was aghast. "Of all the bad things to happen in one family! Please God let us hope and pray he makes a speedy recovery and will be back with you all soon. Have you got any photos of my new little shvesterkind [cousin]? What is her name?"

"Her name is Golda. Here are some pictures of her, and like her name, she has a beautiful head of golden curls and is the cutest little one I have ever seen."

"Leiben on her keppalah [blessing on her head], I cannot wait to meet her and to finally get out of here. I think without Dierdre I would go mad. I just feel I am like in a prison."

The door opened, and his two sisters came in. There was hugging and kissing with their mother and cousin. David had let them know in advance they were coming as they had been visiting him regularly. Zelda was crying with joy. TG her daughters were all right. Their husbands had been in the war but were now home unscathed.

They had brought fruit and chocolates for David, but then one of the sisters, Becky, said, "Oh, by the way, this came for you about a week ago from Marseille, nearly forgot all about it as it was in my pocket."

"Must be from one of my soldier buddies, I will read it later. Thank you."

All mail had been redirected to the sisters when Leon, Zelda, and Hannah moved to England, so this was no surprise. They all just enjoyed the afternoon and the fact they were all together.

Later that day after they all left, Dierdre said, "Come on, David, how about us going for a swim now? And what a lovely afternoon we all had. You have a wonderful family, and now we must look forward to joining them in London with an added bonus of your two sisters Becky and Sarah with their families."

"Yes, it will be wonderful once I can get myself motivated on the sticks. You know, I might have told you I had another sister—Esther. I remember she was very beautiful but died when she was about ten years old with scarlet fever. My parents never got over it.

"Oh, I forgot Becky gave me a letter from Marseille, probably from one of my war buddies. I will read it after we come back . . . Come on, then, my love, let us have a race once we get in the water. I have it down to a fine art now. I sit on the edge and dive in."

After romping in the pool for an hour and a half, Dierdre got him back in his wheelchair and showered while sitting on a chair in the shower. He was more than ready for bed. He lay back on the pillow and felt himself slip into a deep sleep. Dierdre tidied up the room, covered him with a sheet, and then took herself off to her own room, showered, and changed her uniform then went to the cafeteria to have a hot drink. She felt a half-hour rest was in order.

Since she met David, her whole morning, noon, and night centered on him. Never would she have believed how much she could love him, and now feeling his love and their plans for the future gave her the inspiration to carry on each day.

After her refreshment, she put down the magazine she had been reading and made her way back to David's room. He was still asleep, so she sat by his bed quietly and continued to read the book she left always by his bedside. Some time passed, and he began to stir. She bent over and kissed him. "Enough sleep, darling, otherwise you will not sleep tonight! Would you like a nice cup of coffee or tea?"

"I will have some tea, please, and a few biscuits would go down very well, thank you, sweetheart. Oh by the way, in my dressing gown there is that letter. Could you please pass it to me?"

Dierdre handed David the letter and went out to make him some tea; however, when she got back into the room, she saw him crying, so she immediately put the tea down and went over to him, asking, "What is wrong? Are you in pain? Can I help you?"

"I am more in shock than anything. Here, darling, you can read this letter. I have nothing to hide from you."

Dearest David,

> Time has gone by. The war, thank God, is now over. I do not know if you are alive or dead as I have never heard from you.
>
> I am enclosing a picture of our love child. I called her Annabelle. My parents wanted me to have her adopted or even aborted, but I could not do either as this was my only piece of you I could hold on to.
>
> They insisted we move from Paris to Marseille as this brought such shame upon them that people would be talking about them, that they would not be able to hold their heads up. We are in a fishing village. They bought a little shop and began a new life. People believed I was a war widow, and they introduced me to a very wonderful man who absolutely adores Annabelle, so I had to move on and marry him, and now our Annabelle will become a big sister.
>
> My love for you, David, will always live in my heart. I am writing this and sending it to your parents' home so I should try to have

closure in my mind. Always remember I loved you and pray you survived the war.

Madeleine

HYMIE

Months went by. Bertha and Aaron Schubert visited the hospital without seeing their son and just had reports from the doctor: little progress but they were going to give Hymie a new shock treatment and had great confidence that it could help him. Every month, they wrote to Ada, filling her in with whatever the doctor had told them, and as soon as there was any thought of them being allowed in to visit him, they would write her and then she could come over.

Finally on the fifth month, after much despondency and so much distress, the doctor greeted them at the door and said they could visit their son for ten minutes only and warned them he was not yet out of the woods and in fact might not recognize them.

Clutching hold of Aaron's arm, they both went into Hymie's room. He was lying with his face toward the wall. "Zun [son], it is Mutter and Tate."

"Go away. I don't want to see anyone!"

"Tatelah [male child], we have come so far to see you. The doctor said you are doing so much better and you will soon be able to come home and see Ada and your beautiful little girl. Her name is Golda. We have a picture here of them together if you would like to see it."

"No, go away."

They left their son, absolutely heartbroken, and made their way to the doctor's office. Bertha was sobbing, and Aaron said, "Dr. LeRoy, our son did not even want to talk to us. Will he ever get better? He has a wife and baby back in England. How can I ask them to come? What can I write her? Will he ever recuperate?"

"There are no miracles, I am afraid. Your son has been through hell and back, but I am convinced we are making progress. He does not believe he is in a prisoner-of-war camp now, nor does he try to fight the nurses, thinking they are trying to poison him. These are all positive steps in the right direction. Mr. and Mrs. Schubert, you must have patience. I told you when you first came here it could take six months. Now we have this new shock treatment. Write and tell your daughter-in-law it could take possibly a few months more, but she will soon have her husband home with her . . . I would suggest that when he is released from hospital, you have him stay with you for a while until he gets used to being back in the real world, also then you can keep an eye on him."

When they got home, Aaron sat down to write to his daughter-in-law.

Ada, we have just got back from the hospital and had a very good talk with the doctor, who for the very first time allowed us to go in to see Hymie. He would not speak to us at all, which was heartbreaking, but Dr. LeRoy assured us that they had this new shock treatment they were going to administer and that you will soon have your husband home. He suggested that when he will be released, he should first come and stay in our home, simply because it takes time to readjust, as he put it, to the real world. We will leave that up to you to decide when the time comes. Give love to everyone, hugs and kisses to you and Golda.

After receiving this ominous letter, Ada went up to her mother with Golda in her arms. "Mutter, read this. Oy a broch [cannot take anymore]. Who knows if he will ever be normal again? Maybe you will travel with me and Golda when they say they can bring him home. I am so frightened of what will be! If you are with me, at least I will have some confidence. I have to think of Golda, and if he is acting peculiar, I will not stay."

"Calm down, darling girl, come to me. Let me give you a cuddle. You know how much we love you. In the meantime, let me look at Golda. I do not like the look of those spots on her, and yesterday, she was very cranky. Let me feel her keppe [head]. I think she has chickenpox. She is very hot, so go get some cloths and wet them in cold water and we will keep putting them on her to get the fever down nebech [unfortunately], poor little mite."

Ada rushed to get some cloths and did as her mother bade. "Oh, I can never forgive myself not being aware of this. I am so consumed in my mind about Hymie that I think I am going mad. I cannot imagine what he has been through and what they only did to him in that camp. I pray every night that they can make him well again."

"I am sure she will be all right. We will take turns putting the cold cloths on her, and if she is no better in the morning, we will call the doctor. Don't worry. It is a normal thing. You had it when you were five, but it is far worse when adults get it so it is good she has it now."

When Ada got back with a bowl with some wet cloths in it, Hannah went into the kitchen and made an old-fashioned solution to ease the irritation. She came back and started dabbing this wherever she saw a spot on Golda. "This will do until we see the doctor tomorrow. We will send for him straight thing tomorrow morning. Poor little mite, that temperature will soon be normal."

"What are you putting on her? I have never seen that before."

"The old-fashioned methods are always the best. I used it on you and now our precious Golda. I do not write things down, so always remember it:

1 tablespoon of salt
1 tablespoon of baking soda

"Mix them in a dish with water and witch hazel to form a paste. The baking soda will definitely help to take the irritation away, and I am sure when Dr. Cohen comes, he will give us a prescription."

Dr. Arnold Cohen came the following morning. They told him what they had been doing. Golda's temperature had certainly gone back to normal, so he gave them a prescription with strict instructions that this was highly contagious and that they should not go out with her until all the rash had turned into blisters and scabbed. "Also do not be in the company of anyone who is pregnant. Sorry, I must go. We are inundated with people who have the flu. We have an epidemic of Spanish influenza, and unfortunately, it is taking many lives. Don't worry. Little Golda will recover quickly from chickenpox. Keep dabbing the spots with calamine lotion, which I have prescribed, and give her the medicine three times a day."

INFLUENZA OUTBREAK

Dr. Levy was wonderful. He looked in again on Golda on his way home the following evening although he was physically and mentally exhausted. People were dropping like flies with this influenza, which they called the Spanish flu. He had no means to stop this except to warn any member of the family that came down with this all others must wear a mask and wash their hands constantly after touching anything in the room.

That night, Leon came home from work with a raging headache, did not want anything to eat, and went straight to his bed to lie down. Zelda, feeling worried, looked in on him and found him lying fully clothed, but as he did not respond to her, she went over to find him absolutely in a pool of sweat, with a temperature and shivering. Remembering what the doctor had said about wearing a mask and washing their hands, she ran to make something to cover her face with and then returned to try to undress him. It was very difficult as he was a big man, but finally, she managed to half undress him and then get cooling cloths to try to get his temperature down.

It was not easy. She stayed with him all night, not allowing the others into the room. In the morning, she had no other alternative but to send her sister Hannah to get Dr. Levy. Washing her hands constantly, she felt the flood of tears dripping down her face. What if something happened to her darling Leon? He was the one that always took care of everyone else, God bless him. She realized how he had become her life.

When Dr. Levy arrived and examined Leon, shook his head, and confirmed this dreaded disease, he gave Zelda a handful of masks and gave her the warning "Under no conditions must you let the others into the room as this is highly contagious. However, this does not mean he will die. I have no special potion I can give you, except you are doing exactly the right thing to try to get his temperature down. If we can do this, he may stand a chance. I cannot admit him into a hospital. We are inundated, and the staff is at half capacity as they too are coming down with this curse." Dr. Levy said he would look in on Leon the next day. He reached over to Zelda's hand, smiled when he saw the tears in her eyes, and Dr. Levy said, "We must pray."

That night was a nightmare for Zelda. She kept going to get a bowl of cold water, and as she put a cold cloth on Leon, she felt the heat come right out of him into her hand, plus now he was thrashing about in the bed from one side to the other, mumbling incoherently.

"Leon, it is me, Zelda. I am here, darling. I love you so much, and we will fight this, you and I. If you can hear me, know I am right here and will always be by your side. Do not go anywhere, my love. We will get your temperature down. We have made it all this way, Leon, with your hard work. We have always had a good life but now fight harder to get rid of this krankayt [illness]. Oy, a broch [I cannot take anymore]. Don't leave me. Can you hear me? Don't leave me."

Leon lay for three days in and out of a stupor, mumbling and tossing and turning. His temperature was high. Zelda was still trying her best to get it down with damp wet cloths, also trying to moisten his lips as he had not drunk or eaten for all this time and then all of a sudden, he was still. She had been sitting on a chair across the room, and as she neared the bed, a shiver ran through her spine. There was no more breath coming out of him. Zelda sat next to him, holding his hand for what seemed like an eternity and then plucking up the courage to go to her sister and beautiful Ada and tell them this terrible news. She reached their door, and as she went to open it, she collapsed.

Hannah and Ada rushed to her assistance, realizing she was mentally and physically exhausted. Hannah had her head cradled in her lap whilst Ada had some smelling salts and she was waving it under Zelda's nose until she came around. Tears and sobs were flowing as they heard of Leon's death. "Please, Hannah, will you go fetch Dr. Levy? Please also tell him I do not want him to go from a morgue. He will be carried out from our own home. We also have to get in touch with Egerton Road Synagogue so they can make arrangements for the funeral. I also want the rabbi to take the service every night."

Dr. Levy came as soon as he could and pronounced Leon dead and wrote on his death certificate "cause of death: Spanish influenza." The family was in shock, but on hearing which synagogue they belonged to, he said he would inform them. They were so grateful, for he was a real mensch (a person of integrity and honor).

Rabbi Skolnick came to visit them that afternoon, wished them all long life, and said the funeral would take place the following morning in Plashet Cemetery in the East End of London. There would be a service in the synagogue first, and he asked them questions as to what they would like him to say about Leon and if any member would like to speak at that time. Zelda told the rabbi that Sol would speak on behalf of the family and that they would need five shiva chairs as although Harry, Hannah, and Ada were not blood relatives, they felt they wanted to sit as they were mourning very much as Leon considered them his own. Her children in France would not be able to be at the funeral but would sit in their own homes.

The next day, they all congregated in the synagogue. The Rabbi said prayers and gave a speech about Leon, how wonderful he had been in life but this Spanish flu had taken him so quickly from all that loved him, a good man generous to all and he would be so sadly missed, may his dear soul rest in peace.

Sol came over to the podium. "Everyone that is gathered here today knew my father as the type of man that would give you the shirt off his back, so kind and generous he made sure that each one of us had a lovely home to live in. He loved us so much, and we all loved him. My mother and father made us all feel important, and to go to their home, my father was very affectionate and would put his arm around us and give us a big hug and kiss. I can only tell you that his passing has left a huge hole in all our hearts. My sisters Esther, Becky, and Sarah will sit shiva in France, and my poor brother David is in a rehabilitation hospital in France minus two legs. My father's dream was to bring them all over, but I as his oldest son will try my best to fulfill his wishes." After that, he then said Kaddish (the mourners' prayer). There was not a dry eye in the room.

After the service, all the women walked back to Filey Avenue, the men to the burial grounds. One of the neighbors brought in a large urn, which they filled with water and heated up for tea when the men came back. They had ordered big platters of small bagels and bridge rolls, beautifully done with smoked salmon, egg salad, cream cheese, and white fish; each was decorated with either pickled cucumber or tomatoes.

The synagogue was overflowing with people, as Leon was so well known in the trade that all his customers and suppliers all came to pay their respects;

however, those who could not be at the funeral could offer their condolences at the shiva, where they would all be for the week.

As the men came back after the funeral, they washed their hands in a place provided for them outside the door as was the custom. They were all famished. It had been a long hot schlep (to go with effort).

Sol went over to his mother, putting his arms about her. "Darling, dearest Mother, know that I will be by your side for all the days that I live, and I know my wonderful father is now resting in peace." Then he took his seat beside his mother. Someone came over to him and put a plate of food in his hand. Another came over and placed a little table in front of him and then brought him a cup of tea. Everything was a complete blur. People were coming over to him and the family, wishing them long life, and then the rabbi came back in the early evening for evening services.

The family felt they could not cry anymore. Their eyes were red and swollen, but with every friend, relative, or neighbor, plus workers or suppliers and shopkeepers, the tears came rolling down as each had such a special story of Leon.

One was saying how bad this Spanish flu was, how it was all over the world, and said one of their children had come home from school and repeated the song they were singing:

> I had a little bird, its name was Enza,
> I opened the window and influenza.

"The teachers are telling the children to go home, tell their mothers to disinfect everything and use carbolic soap, which is an antiseptic and the smell of which would help to keep any germs away."

When the last person left for that evening, they all retired to their bedrooms. Sol said he would spend the night there, and they were all physically and mentally exhausted. No one had a chance to look at the mail today, but Ada noticed there was a letter from Bertha and Aaron Schubert to say they had been to the hospital that day and the doctor said, "Hymie is now communicating, and he will be best in his own environment."

"So, mamaleh [endearment], whenever you can come with little Golda, we are sure it will help with his recovery to see his loved ones."

Ada immediately wrote back to say, "It is impossible for us to come right now. Golda has just had the chickenpox, and I am now sitting shiva for my Uncle Leon, who as you know I always considered my father as he literally brought me up, as I never knew my real father. I will not go into all that now as you know that story, but when I come, it will be in approximately a month. I will come with my mother and my aunt as I could not possibly leave them alone after this nightmare.

"Sending my love to you, kiss my husband for me, and let him know we love him."

The week went round like a whirlwind. Everyone was very kind and sent in platters of food, and when it was all over, they all felt deflated, and that was when Ada told them of the letter she had received from the Schuberts and hoped they would travel with her in a month to see them as they had brought Hymie home and at last, he was communicating.

Zelda was in a terrible state, crying all the time and in a deep depression that Hannah felt she had to call Dr. Levy in to see her as she kept saying she did not want to live anymore. Yes, they all felt Leon's loss, but this was too much to bear. Little Golda kept going over to her great-aunt with her dollies, but when the doctor came, he spoke sharply to her and said, "Zelda, thank God you have a wonderful family. You are very much alive, and they need you so much. Your son will be coming back to you. He needs all your strength and encouragement, not you crying night and day. I am prescribing something for you to calm yourself down, which will help you sleep."

"Ada tells me that Hymie is now with his parents but Hannah and Ada will not travel without you, so when you are feeling better, you have something nice to look forward to. You will go with them and visit your children and grandchildren. Life goes on, my dear, and you are so lucky to have such a supportive and loving family."

It was six weeks before Zelda found the strength to say, "All right, let us book the passage going over. We will not book a return voyage back as we will wait and see. I may stay with the girls for a little while, but depending on how David is coming along, if he is ready to come over to England, I will go with them. On the other hand, you, Ada, may not want to stay with Hymie's parents, and you may feel he is ready mentally to come back with you. Oh, I do hope so."

This was like the old Zelda. Hannah got so excited she got up and crossed the room and gave her sister a big kiss and hug.

GOING HOME

Booking the ferry for the following week seemed to bring new life into Zelda. They all got ready for their voyage although short. The English Channel was certainly not anything to look forward to. Ada was like a bear with a sore head. Hannah said, "Take no notice of her. She is just so anxious about Hymie, plus she has her period. I try to feel for her, but I can only guess what she is going through mentally. And will he be all right with little Golda? Remember he has never seen her before."

"Don't worry. We have to accept in life what will be will be. I cannot believe what happened to you, a beautiful, wonderful girl left with three children, and now me. At least I had all those years with poor Leon, God rest his soul, and now I am a widow," upon which she burst into tears. Hannah went over to her sister, and they put their arms around each other and tried to console themselves, each with their own thoughts.

After a few days, Wednesday came around. They were all getting themselves ready and organized. Ada was shouting at Golda to stop running around so she could comb her hair, when Hannah stepped in and said, "Don't worry, darling. I will get her ready. You look after yourself and make sure you have everything you need. I am all ready now, so I have time."

They had a hansom cab arranged to take them to the train, and then they would go straight onto the ferry. Golda was very excited and wanted to bring her dolls, but they said they were going a very long way so she could only bring one; however, they promised her they would definitely buy her a French doll after they arrived.

Once on the boat, Ada and Golda were terribly sick from the up-and-down motion; however, Zelda and Hannah seemed fine. Zelda said, "I am so looking forward to seeing David and Dierdre. The last we heard from them, he was doing so much better, so I hope he will be able to come to London very soon. Nebech [unfortunately] he has been through so much. I am so thankful he met Dierdre, who will always look after him and, most important, love him."

The journey seemed endless, but eventually, the ship landed and they embarked on French soil. Mr. Schubert had arranged for a hansom cab to pick them up from the docks, which they were very thankful for and they blessed Ada's in-laws for being so thoughtful. No doubt they were concerned because they now had Hymie home. What would his reaction be when he saw Ada and, most of all, their precious little Golda?

Finally, they reached the house. It was a beautiful sunny day, and when they knocked on the door, there was Bertha with a wide smile on her face and with open arms. She hugged them and ushered them into the house. "You must be starving, so I have made you plenty to eat. Come, come. Aaron, take their coats and let us all get comfortable. I am sorry Hymie is not down to see you. He is sleeping right now as he still gets so very tired. I think mainly because of the medication they have given him for depression. Wait until he sees our beautiful Golda. My goodness, what hair she has. She is like a little doll."

They all took turns in going to the bathroom to freshen themselves up. Ada put on some lipstick and a little rouge and fluffed up her hair as she wanted to make sure she looked pretty for Hymie. She really did not know what to expect after all this time. Would he even know who she was, and what would his reaction be to Golda? Ada's thoughts were running wild. She felt her stomach churning in anticipation to see her husband, and yes, disappointment that he was actually not there to meet them as they arrived.

She put a smile on her face as she reentered the dining room. Everyone turned to look at her, and Hannah said, "Darling, you look so beautiful."

"My daughter-in-law has always looked beautiful, but today, Ada, you look radiant. Come sit around the table and let us fress [eat]. Hymie will not be down for about an hour, and you must all be starving hungry." Bertha was pushing a plate into Ada's hand and telling her to put some food on the plate that she thought Golda might like to eat. She believed she felt just as nervous as Ada looked.

After about an hour of small talk, Ada was wringing her hands, and Bertha could see that she was clinging to her mother, so she said, "I am going up to see my son. It is about time he was here to see his beautiful family. Since he has been out of the hospital he has needed his rest, but once he sees you, Ada and Golda, I am sure he will be back to his normal self."

She left the room, and within minutes, there was the most piercing scream. Aaron rushed out of the room and up the stairs to find Bertha collapsed, unconscious on the landing. With Hymie's door wide open, he saw his son hanging. "Oh my God, why did you do it? Oh my God, why oh why?" He went over to Bertha but could not do anything for her for the moment.

Ada was shouting up. "What is wrong? Do you want me to come up?" Aaron put a pillow under Bertha's head and then went down to say what had happened. Getting a knife, he went back up to cut Hymie down and gave his wife some smelling salts when she came to. She was hysterical.

Aaron told Ada and her family that he did not want anyone to see Hymie like that. Ada made her mother-in-law a cup of tea, but she could see she was shaking so much. They all huddled together, crying in each other's arms, so much so that Golda started to cry too. Aaron rushed out to the police station; he really did not know what to do first.

Zelda made a decision that she would ask Ada if she could take Golda to her daughters so she would never have bad memories of this, and this way, Hannah could stay with her daughter because of course she would have to sit shiva with her in-laws. What a terrible experience for everyone. Ada could not stop crying and saying how much she loved him. "My life is finished. I cannot go on."

"Of course, you can go on. You have a child, and she is dependent upon you to be strong for her, like I was for you, my darling. You knew you always had your mother. I will say something to you in Yiddish that someone said to me when your father left me: Der mensch trakht un Gott lakht [man plans and God laughs]. Let Zelda take Golda to her daughters. I will stay with you, and as much as your heart aches, so does his mother's and father's."

The police came, examined everything, and took pictures of the scene, after which an ambulance arrived and they took Hymie to the mortuary. The rabbi was marvelous, very comforting and soothing. He was so very sympathetic. Hymie would not be buried as was the tradition the next day, as there was to be an inquest, after which they would be informed as to when that would be and then they could sit shiva (mourning).

"Momma, I will not leave you. I will stay with you for as long as you need me and maybe now you will both sell up and come to London so you can be near us and watch Golda grow up. I cannot bear to think of leaving you both here anyway. Perhaps you can think about it." Bertha was still hysterical, and when the doctor came, he gave both Bertha and Ada a tranquilizer and told them both to lie down and try to sleep.

Aaron too was beside himself, but Hannah was there to talk to him and make him eat and she spoke to him about coming to England. "Try to persuade Bertha to come. We are your family, Aaron, and what have you got, nightmare memories living in this house. If you are in England, at least you will be able to see your grandchild growing up. I know how hard it is for you, but it will be doubly hard for Bertha. Hymie, God rest his soul, was all Ada could talk about. She loved him to the moon and back."

"How can I tell you this, Hannah? But I must. I never told Bertha, but I used to sit with Hymie quietly in his room and talk to him. One day he put his arms around me and sobbed and sobbed. He said they put him in a room all by himself and used him like a woman, and in between his sobs, he kept saying he was so ashamed he wanted to die. I think the thought of seeing Ada again made him so distraught within himself that suicide was the only way out. I do not want you to tell Ada, Hannah. This conversation is just between us."

Hannah put her arms around him to comfort him, and Aaron could not stop crying. Hannah kept patting him on the shoulder and said, "You have had a tremendous shock, and I understand after what he went through that he could not face life. Aaron, this house will have terrible memories for you. You have such a beautiful granddaughter, and if you sell up and come to London, both you and Bertha will have the joy of seeing Golda grow up, plus you will have all of us if you can stand us." And for once, she saw a little smile on his face.

"I will speak to Bertha about it once she feels a little better."

"We will stay with you and help you through this difficult time. Ada will sit shiva with you, and I suggest you put this house on the market, sell up after that, and live close by us. Remember whatever you discussed with me stays schtum [silent]. I will never breathe a word!"

The week passed by so slowly. Neighbors were coming in and out, bringing platters of food so no one had to cook or think about shopping, which Hannah was very grateful for. She passed her time speaking of Golda, showing her pictures, and making the conversation as light as possible as everyone seemed to want to speak about Hymie, and every time the conversation turned to him, Ada ran out of the room, crying. Bertha sat as if in a daze, never uttering a word except to say what a good boy he had been. It was absolutely heartbreaking!

After a month, Bertha agreed it was a good idea and that they would move to England. They left the house in the hands of an agent, and they traveled back with Hannah and Ada. Zena still was looking after Golda, and they were staying with her daughters as David would be able to move with Dierdre in a month, so hopefully, they would be able to all come together. In the meantime, Bertha and Aaron would be able to stay in Filey Avenue until they found a place.

When they arrived in London, they stayed in Filey Avenue with the family, but at once put their names down with agents around the area to view a house or flat of their own. Ada was delighted so she could keep an eye on her in-laws. She loved them very much, and although she too was heartbroken, there was a mission in her life now to see them settled and to see them be the grandparents they deserved to be, and for them to get some happiness from their granddaughter they richly needed.

Morris and Son was their agent, and their representative came round to them two weeks after their arrival, a very nice young man who said they had a flat vacant at the end of the month, nice and roomy, and he thought they should have a look at it. This apartment was right on Stamford Hill, on top of the grocery shop, with two bedrooms, a nice-size lounge, and a kitchen. Ada got very excited, so she persuaded them to at least have a look at it. Bertha and Issac said they would go the next day and Ada would go with them to look at it.

"Momma and Poppa, it may be ideal for you, so keep an open mind. We will look at all options, and in the meantime, your house in France has not sold so this could be a stopgap."

When they arrived, Boris Shapiro introduced himself to them. He was the agent for Morris and Sons, a very nice, presentable man, and he showed them around the flat, also the fact that it was nicely decorated and it had a small garden in the back, where one could have a line out for their washing to dry. "Oh my," Bertha said, "I will be so close to you, darling Ada. This is so nice and bright. Look, the sun is shining. This is all a good sign." But looking at Boris, she said, "How much is this a week?"

"If you like this apartment, the owners of the shop want to have people in that would be responsible and not loud, so their asking rent is only one pound per week, with a one-year lease."

"I do not have to look anywhere else, darling Ada. We can make this our home for now, and at least we will be so close to you all we will not be lonely. I know you will see to that."

"I am so happy, Momma. It has all worked out at a fantastic time as David and Dierdre arrive this week and we are going to change the whole ground floor for him so he does not have any stairs to worry about. God bless Dierdre, she looks after him like a baby, but once he is settled, she is going back to work as she is a nurse."

Time just seemed to fly by. It took a full month to get David settled. They had everything they could possibly need. Dierdre saw to everything for him, and once she got herself the job in the Prince of Wales general hospital in Tottenham, North London, she was able to get a tram down from Stamford Hill and not be too far from home.

David was so appreciative of the family. They included him in everything, and he just loved being with little Golda, calling her his little Goldilocks. He read to her and played all sorts of games with her, so whenever she was home, she went straight to his room. She just loved her Uncle David as the whole family did. Sol in the factory brought home each night paperwork for David to keep the books, which he was brilliant at and kept him busy so he was not bored.

Hannah received a letter from Morris in America. They sent photographs regularly, but this time, he was insisting his mother come to visit, and yes, bring Ada. After all, she had been through so much, this would be good for her. She could bring Goldie, as they called her and not Golda. After all, he said that she had never seen her grandchildren and now they were expecting their fourth. "Being very religious, I cannot imagine how many they will have, so many thoughts going through her mind," Morris said. "Let me know, Momma. I will send the tickets and let me tell you, I will be so excited!"

When Hannah approached the subject with Ada, a look of dismay came across her face. "Momma, I would love to go with you to see Morris and his family, but I just could not leave my in-laws unless I speak to them and possibly leave Golda with them. I will see them tomorrow and ask them what is best. As you know, I have been going there every day, and just being with Golda has become their whole life. That is the only thing that makes them happy."

Hannah went over to her daughter and, putting her arms around her, said, "Darling, you have been through so much, and a break away would also do you a world of good."

"We will see, Momma. I am going to bed now, and tomorrow is another day."

Going to her in-laws the following day, Ada could not believe how happy they were that she could entrust little Golda into their care so she could go visit her brother and family without worrying. They would pick her up from nursery as Golda was now four years old and, at least once a week, would take her to see the family in Filey Avenue. When Ada told her mother this news, she immediately wrote to Morris that she would be coming with Ada and that her in-laws were going to look after Golda.

All was good in London. They could go away with peace of mind. Aunt Zelda was in correspondence with her daughters. They were trying to sell up in France so they could eventually come to England, and somehow or other, they would all manage for a while until they got settled. It would not be easy, but Sol said he would have the children stay at his house. The grown-ups would just make do. Zelda said, "I will be so happy to have my wonderful family around me."

The day arrived for Hannah and Ada to go. Crying with happiness, they waved their farewells.

ABOUT THE AUTHOR

I, Adele Sinoway/Barnett, was born in London and, throughout the war years, was evacuated to Ilfracombe, North Devon.

I have had a very colorful life. My two sons were born in New Zealand. I traveled to both Panama and Tahiti going there on a cargo ship, and while returning to England, I visited both Australia and South Africa. I now am an American citizen living in New Jersey, and I have resided so for the last forty-five years.

This is my first novel, which I hope to make into a trilogy.

ABOUT THE BOOK

Saga of Generations is a family story of Jewish people, some who escaped the horrific murderous ways of Russia taking place in 1818, going through generations over four continents, including the World War I, this book includes love, lust, and heartache. Read and you will feel that each of these characters is part of your family.

Lightning Source UK Ltd.
Milton Keynes UK
UKHW010311080223
416649UK00009B/148/J